THE
LEGACY
A NOVEL

JUDITH BLEVINS

Judith Blevins

Brass Frog Bookworks
www.BrassFrogBookworks.com

2764 Compass Drive Suite 203-3
Grand Junction, CO 81506

THE LEGACY
Copyright © 2014 by Judith Blevins. All Rights Reserved.

This is a work of fiction. The character names, places, entities and in-
cidents are a product of the author's imagination or, if real, used ficti-
tiously.

The opinions expressed by the author are not necessarily those of Brass
Frog Bookworks™

Published by
BRASS FROG BOOKWORKS™ Independent Publishers
2764 Compass Drive Suite 203-3 | Grand Junction, CO 81506|
909-239-0344 or 970-434-9361| *www.BrassFrogBookworks.com*

Brass Frog Bookworks is dedicated to excellence and integrity in the
publishing industry. The company was founded on the belief in the
power of language and the spiritual nature of human creativity. "In the
beginning was the Word…" John 1:1

Book design copyright © 2014 by Brass Frog Bookworks™
All rights reserved.

Cover & Interior Design:
Blue Harvest Creative (*www.blueharvestcreative.com*)

Inquiries should be addressed to:

Judith Blevins
Fountainhead Blvd. G-8
Grand Junction, CO 81505

Printed in the United States of America | First Printing 2014
Library of Congress Control Number: 2014954570
ISBN: 978-0-9899412-7-3

1. Fiction/Romance   2. Fiction/Paranormal   3. Fiction/Suspense

OTHER TITLES BY JUDITH BLEVINS

DOUBLE JEOPARDY

Love blows into Farmington like the searing desert wind when high school friends, Nick and Jas, are reunited after many long years. The spark between them is soon fanned into an inferno of passion. Grateful to have a second chance at happiness, they dream of a life together. But their private demons are too much. When Jas begins to doubt Nick, a force is ignited that will forever change the course of their lives. Jas has blood on her hands. Is she a cold-blooded murderer? Follow the intriguing events as they unfold and spiral wildly out of control, culminating in an incredible, unexpected conclusion.

SWAN SONG

Kara Isabella is smart, beautiful, and rich. Her family connections made landing a job with the Spanish Embassy at the United Nations as easy as a well-placed phone call. When she crosses paths with presidential hopeful, Senator Mark Langford, he is immediately captivated, particularly by her family's wealth and power. With high hopes, Langford pursues the lovely Spaniard. But, his appetite for beautiful women becomes a snare when one lover meets a gruesome death, and Kara learns of his deceit. Just when he thinks he has landed a trophy wife and a certain path to the White House, his plan and his life unravel. As he struggles to escape potential scandal, a blackmailer haunts him from the shadows. Will he be able to hold onto his bid for the White House? Follow the twists and turns in this tale of intrigue, treachery and death. Just when you think you have it figured out; the shocking ending will leave you breathless.

*To those who were instrumental
in forming my legacy, my ancestors …*

ACKNOWLEDGEMENTS

Special thanks to fellow fiction writer, Carroll Multz, for his encouragement, editing skills, inspiration, advice and for graciously allowing me to use the lyrics to his original musical compositions in this novel.

Also, my thanks and grateful appreciation to my publisher, Patti Hoff, for her expertise and guidance, and Debbie Brockett, for her expert editing skills.

THE PROGRAM

Time heals almost everything. Give it time.

Author Unknown

MOVEMENT ONE
INTERMEZZO

CHAPTER 1

KABOOM! Thunder roared as a bolt of lightning streaked across the black sky, and the rain began in earnest. It was early spring in southern Louisiana, and torrential downpours were expected. The thunder competed with Grant Alexander's singing, and lightning illuminated the Lincoln's interior. Caroline leaned closer to Grant, her husband of three years, and slid her hand along his thigh. Grant squeezed her hand in reply, transmitting an unspoken promise. He continued to sing *O Sole Mio*, as he steered the car with his left hand and imitated conducting an orchestra with his right. He was on a personal high having received a standing ovation after performing his piano concerto with the Westchester Philharmonic Symphony Orchestra of New Orleans, earlier that evening.

New Orleans was a playground for the rich and famous, and Thompson Sinclair, CEO of *Spinners, Inc.*, a recording conglomerate based in San Diego, had been in the audience. Grant hoped his piano solo might launch him into a recording career if Sinclair liked his music. Grant recognized his talent was exceptional, and the audience confirmed that with the standing ovation. Even Edwardo Ponzetti, the conductor, bowed to Grant at the conclusion of his solo—a gesture the orchestra seldom witnessed.

"Be careful, Grant. The rain is coming down so hard; perhaps we should pull over and wait it out. We could stay in a hotel and spend a romantic night together." Caroline said.

"I have it all under control, my dear wife. I don't want to stay in a hotel; however, I'll take you up on that romantic night suggestion when we get home," Grant answered. "Damn weather! You would think it would cooperate and be as spectacular as my performance was tonight."

Caroline noticed Grant was gripping the steering wheel very tightly. "Yes, Grant," she said, as she peered through the windshield.

"As it is, I can barely see the road," Grant said, squinting. He leaned forward and searched for the center stripe. "The rain is so heavy the windshield wipers can hardly handle the downpour."

"Are you sure it's wise to continue?" Caroline asked, in a shaky voice.

Grant had quit singing and was studying the road, carefully. "Quiet! I have to concentrate."

Suddenly, the vehicle fishtailed on the wet pavement and careened toward the shoulder.

"Son-of-a-bitch!" Grant cried, fighting the steering wheel trying to stabilize the car.

"Grant!" Caroline screamed. Her husband whipped the wheel first one way and then the other, but his efforts to regain control were in vain. The Lincoln tore through the guard rail and shimmied onto the muddy shoulder.

Caroline screamed, again. She hadn't fastened her seatbelt and was being tossed about like a rag doll. Grant continued to turn the steering wheel trying to gain leverage, as they careened off the shoulder of the road.

"Oh, God," Grant cried, seeing a giant oak tree looming before them. He instinctively reached over and pulled Caroline into him an instant before impact. The vehicle slammed into the tree, twisting metal and shattering glass. It rebounded from the injured bark and then jolted its unconscious cargo to a rest.

THE OCCUPANTS in the car travelling behind the Alexander vehicle witnessed the accident. The driver pulled over and turned on the emergency flashers.

"Looks like a bad one," he shouted over the rain pelting the roof of their Subaru. Drs. Stephen and Eleanor Monroe grabbed their medical bags from the rear seat and hastened to render aid. Stephen, upon reaching the driver's side, shouted to Eleanor, "Oh, my God. It's Grant and Caroline Alexander. I think Grant may be dead." Stephen was Grant's longtime physician and recognized him instantly, although Grant's face was bloody from a gash in his forehead.

Eleanor, in the meantime, had gone around to the passenger side of the wrecked Lincoln. Caroline lay motionless in a twisted position, covered with blood. Eleanor took a deep breath and carefully put her arm through the broken glass of the passenger window. She found Caroline's wrist and searched for a pulse.

"Caroline is alive, but badly injured!" Eleanor shouted. "She's losing a lot of blood. It's coming from a nasty gash on her neck but, thank God, it isn't the jugular. An ambulance isn't going to cut it. I'll call for Life Flight helicopter."

Eleanor stepped away from the car, pulled her cell phone from her jacket pocket, and hastily dialed 911.

"This is 911. What's the nature of your emergency?"

"Operator, my name is Dr. Eleanor Monroe. There's been an accident on Highway Six, at mile marker sixteen, a few miles from the French Quarter. We have critical injuries and are requesting a life flight, as soon as possible."

"I'm calling it in, now. Stay on the line."

"Thank you."

"I got a confirmation. They're ten to fifteen minutes out."

"We may not have that much time."

"I'll relay that to the medical team. God be with you."

"Thanks for your help…and your prayers."

Eleanor tapped her cell phone and jammed it back into her pocket. Since the passenger door was partially opened from the force of the impact, she squeezed through and set about doing a more thorough examination of the injured woman.

"I'll try to slow the bleeding," she shouted, "but, at this rate, she won't last long. I don't think the chopper will get here soon enough to save her." She looked across at Stephen, whose grim features matched her own. He looked down at his patient and shook his head.

The Lincoln's driver side door was gaping, hanging from a hinge. Grant's body had slammed into the steering wheel and was draped over it. Stephen had eased him back against the seat and brushed glass off his tuxedo. Pulling his handkerchief out of his pants pocket, he gently dabbed at the blood on Grant's face. His face was white underneath. Stephen retrieved his stethoscope from his medical bag and, after doing a cursory examination, looked at his wife.

"He's beyond our help. I'd guess he has massive internal injuries after slamming into the steering wheel." Leaning into the car, he scrounged around in the backseat. "Do we have anything in our car that we can use as a canopy?"

"I'll look, but I doubt it," Eleanor said. She backed out into the rain and headed for their Subaru. She slipped in the mud and landed on her knee. "Damn!"

Stephen shouted after her, "While you're at it, pull the car up closer. We need more light."

Eleanor swiped at her muddy Italian wool slacks, without much success. "Good idea. Let me find a cover, first."

Minutes later, Eleanor pulled the brake on their car, its headlights cutting a swath through the near horizontal streaks of rain. She stepped out, opening a large blue and white striped umbrella Stephen used when playing golf.

"I found this in the back," Eleanor said. "Will it do?"

"Yes, it'll do nicely. Can you hold it while I extricate Grant?"

Eleanor propped the umbrella against the open driver's door, positioning it in such a way as to shield Grant's limp body from the downpour. Stephen pulled Grant from the wreckage and laid him on the wet grass beside the Lincoln.

"I don't believe it. I just saw him, yesterday. He gave me our tickets to the symphony." Stephen placed his fingers on Grant's neck, once again.

"Hey!" He shifted his position so he was closer. "There's a heartbeat!" He looked up at his wife. "But, it's really faint."

Eleanor massaged her brow with her thumb and forefinger, wondering whether to share a thought that had occurred to her. Kneeling beside her husband, she asked, "Stephen, if…if Grant doesn't make it…you know, if there's nothing we can do for him…we may be able to save Caroline. If we act, quickly. I slowed her bleeding down, but she desperately needs a transfusion."

Stephen put his hand on her shoulder. "Eleanor, what are you suggesting?"

She rose and hurried back to the passenger side of the Lincoln. She found Caroline's black evening bag and dumped the contents out, searching for a driver's license.

"Stephen, she's AB positive," Eleanor exclaimed, holding the license up. "You and I are both A. Do you remember Grant's blood type?"

"Yes. He's type O positive, universal." He placed his own jacket under the bleeding man's head. "Easy to remember. Why?"

Eleanor returned to her husband's side. She observed her husband gently wiping blood from Grant's face with those miraculous hands of his. She had assisted Stephen with numerous surgeries during her internship at Immaculate Heart of Mary Hospital, in New Orleans, and was in awe of his surgical skill. As they worked side-by-side, their professional relationship had grown into romance, and they'd fallen in love. They were married soon after Eleanor completed her internship. Eleanor believed in predestination; they were meant to be together.

Pushing her musings to the back of her mind, Eleanor sighed. "If we could jerry-rig a transfusion line between the two of them, while Grant's heart is still beating, we may be able get enough of his blood into her to save her life." She scrutinized the expression on Stephen's face and pushed forward. "What do you think?"

Stephen swiped rain from his eyes. He regarded his dying friend and then his wife, his brilliant, amazing wife. "By God, it's worth a try. What have we got to lose?"

Eleanor nodded briskly. "Our license to practice comes to mind…" She suddenly started shivering, whether from the rain or from stress she couldn't decide. She tightened the belt on her coat and helped her husband up.

Stephen said, emphatically, "We very well could, but can we live with letting someone die because we're afraid of the consequences? We took the Hippocratic Oath. Saving lives is our job, so… let's get on with it."

Trying to hide a smile, Eleanor said, "Yes, let's." Rain-soaked and still shivering, she took the medical bags to the rear of the wreck, where she could see better in the beam of the Subaru's headlights. She searched for anything they could use to establish a transfusion line.

In the interim, Stephen returned to the passenger side of the Lincoln and squeezed in. Leaning into the back seat, he found a Saints stadium blanket and, wrapping it around Caroline, he gently picked her up and carried her to the driver's side of the car. He laid her next to her husband.

Eleanor, who had completed her search of the medical bags, approached and said, "Look, I found these. Do you think they'll work?" She showed him three packages of sterile catheters, surgical clamps, hypodermic syringes, and alcohol wipes. "Not too fancy, but…"

Stephen peered at the items and shook his head. "Do you have a miracle tucked away in that collection?"

"Dearest, I've seen you perform miracles. It's in your DNA. You *can* do this; I know you can, even if the odds are stacked against us."

Stephen peeled off Grant's jacket and ripped open his shirt. "With that kind of faith, how can I miss?" Fumbling in the dying man's pants pocket, Stephen found a clean handkerchief which he applied as a tourniquet.

Eleanor set about sterilizing the man's arm with alcohol swabs, as Stephen began to prepare Caroline. The doctors worked feverishly for several minutes and finally had a make-shift transfusion line hooked between the arms of Caroline and Grant.

"Okay, partner, say a prayer and, just to be on the safe side, cross your fingers. I'm concerned that we don't have a sterile enough environment to work in, but, what the hell! If we don't do something, they're both dead, anyway." With that, Stephen removed the tourniquet from Grant's arm and the blood began flowing, slowly at first, but when Stephen started a gentle CPR, the flow increased.

After a few minutes, while monitoring a blood pressure cuff, Eleanor said, "You are a genius! Her blood pressure is rising!"

"That's good to hear." The relief in Stephen's voice was evident. "I had my doubts," he muttered, as he continued the CPR. "And, my love, you're the genius. This was your idea. You're the brains, I'm just the brawn."

"This may have been a long shot, Stephen but never underestimate your skill. Not many MDs would have even attempted such a feat, much less successfully."

Before Stephen could answer, they heard the flap, flap, flap of the blades, as the rescue chopper approached.

Eleanor stood up and began waving her arms at the chopper. Stephen sat back on his heels, rubbing his aching arms. He was cold and wet. He put his fingers on Grant's neck looking for that faint pulse, but found none.

"He's dead," he shouted to Eleanor. Then he leaned closer to Caroline looking for signs of life. He heard her groan, as he touched her wrist. Jerking his head up, he looked at Eleanor who was still waving at the chopper.

I think she's going to be all right, dear! She's weak and a little hoarse, but she just whispered that she was going to live. Her exact words were, 'I will live on.'"

"Now that's what I call determination," Eleanor replied, as she joined her husband at Caroline's side, and the doctors grasped hands. Eleanor made the sign of the cross and looking heavenward, said, "Dear God, bless Grant and take his soul to heaven and into your loving arms. Thank you for the miracle we prayed for. Now, at least, Caroline has a fighting chance."

The chopper was on the ground and the flight crew was running towards them. Stephen removed the makeshift transfusion line and took Grant's arms, carefully folding them across his chest. Placing his hands over Grant's, he looked up at his wife. "What a shame. These hands will never play the piano, again."

Eleanor nodded. "An amazing talent lost forever."

CHAPTER
2

THREE MONTHS LATER

Having just been released from the hospital and returning home to the mansion she had shared with Grant, Caroline stood before the mirror in the foyer. She couldn't remember how many surgeries she had undergone and, afterward, all of the reconstruction. Outwardly, she looked the same. Inwardly she was different.

"Why do I feel so...so disconnected, Paul? Like I'm a stranger in my own home. Now, I understand that 'out of body feeling' I've heard others talk about."

"It's to be expected." Dr. Paul Bruno was Caroline's psychiatrist as well as being an old family friend. He was like an uncle to her. In fact, as a child she only knew him as Uncle Paul. As an adult, she'd dropped the "Uncle" part, though he remained a father figure to her. Paul had gone to West Point with her father, Winston Schumann, who was known among his intimates as The Senator. He'd served South Carolina as senator for four terms.

Paul slipped his arms into the sleeves of his raincoat, preparing to leave. "You've experienced a lot of trauma, my dear girl. Losing Grant and fighting for your own life has taken its toll on you, both mentally and physically, but you'll start to feel like your old self before long."

He looked affectionately down the cozy, wood paneled hallway into the drawing room beyond. "I will always have a vision of Grant sitting at his ebony baby grand." He shook his head, as if to loosen the memory. Running his fingers through his thick gray hair, he assured Caroline, "Being in familiar surroundings will help. Just be patient and take time to heal. I'll drop by tomorrow to see how you're doing." Paul pulled on his black leather driving gloves and sauntered toward the door.

"Looks like it may rain, all day," he observed, as a cool moist breeze swept through the open doorway.

Paul leaned down and gave Caroline a kiss on the forehead. "You know you can call me anytime—day or night," he said, and then dashed through the rain toward his Lexus, parked in the driveway.

"I know," Caroline called after him from the edge of the veranda. "I will, I promise."

Caroline reentered the mansion and closed the door behind her. She leaned back against it

and looked down the corridor, towards the drawing room. Her gaze settled on the piano positioned
in front of a large window overlooking the patio
and pool. Tears filled her eyes, as she recalled that
it was where Grant had spent most of his time,
filling the house with melodious measures meant
for her alone. The music often preluded a night of
wild lovemaking. There was nothing as sexy as a
concerto created just for you.

*Oh, Grant, everything reminds me of you. Every-
thing I touch and everything I see. I even think I hear
you whispering. The moment I returned home, I've
had this urge to play your piano. You know I've rarely
played! I wouldn't know a high C from a low C, if my
life depended on it. Is this something I'm feeling to keep
me connected to you? Why couldn't I have been the one
that died? You had so much to live for and, now that
you're gone, my life is turned topsy-turvy. Sometimes I
feel as though I'm going mad. You were my everything.
What am I to do with myself, now?*

Caroline wandered into the drawing room,
reluctantly approaching the piano. Grant's piano.
She edged herself onto the bench, and suddenly
memories flooded her mind. As if in a dream, she
placed her hands on the keys and began to play. The
arrangement was the concerto Grant had played the
night he died. Her untaught fingers danced lithely
across the keys, and she played as mesmerizing as
Grant had that rainy, fateful, awful night.

Caroline suddenly realized she was doing the
impossible and tried to pull her hands away from

the keys, but the piece played on. Something was holding her hostage. When the music stopped, her hands were relinquished, and she jumped up, knocking the bench over. Sheet music scattered across the carpet.

What the—am I losing my mind? I didn't just do that, did I? What just happened? She slammed the keyboard cover down and fled from the room. She swiftly ascended the stairs to her bedroom and locked the door. In the bathroom, she fumbled in the medicine cabinet for a prescription bottle of sedatives. Finally, she had it in her hand. Struggling to get the cap off, she eventually was able to down a double dose. Taking a deep breath, she collapsed onto the rose satin coverlet. Within minutes, she was fast asleep.

CAROLINE'S SLUMBER was not restful. She tossed and turned and moaned, as she dreamt that Grant spoke to her.

Caroline, even though I'm no longer of the physical world, we're still connected. You received more than my blood in the transfusion. You also received a part of my soul. Through you, I will still be a famous concert pianist. My music will be heard throughout the world. Although it will be you sitting at the piano, it will be me who will be playing. Together, we will set the world on fire!

Caroline began murmuring. *No, no, no. Please go away. You're not Grant. Grant is dead. Whoever you are, please go away.*

"Don't you realize it is me, your loving husband, Grant?"

"But…but, I don't know how to play."

"Just put your hands on the keys and I'll do the rest."

The grandfather clock in the foyer chimed five times, startling Caroline. She jerked upright. Her heart was pounding. She looked around the room searching for Grant.

"Grant, are you here? I feel your presence. I had a strange dream that you talked to me. Please. Answer me." After a few seconds, she realized she was still half asleep and felt foolish conversing with her dead husband. *I'm really losing it. I could have sworn Grant was here. Oh, God, what's happening to me? Please tell me I was just hallucinating.* She slid back down into the warm hollow of the bed sheets and pulled the coverlet up around her neck. She could hardly keep her eyes open.

THE NEXT morning, Caroline was up early. She still felt that Grant had been there the night before, but knew that was impossible. *I'm stressed and imagining things. I need to find something to do to keep me occupied. I bet it was the lullaby pills. No wonder my pharmacist advised against taking too many.* Remembering Paul and his offer to call him, anytime, she picked up the phone and dialed his home number.

"Caroline! Is everything all right?" Paul asked, anxiously.

"Yes. Well, not really. I need to get out for a while. Will you be in your office, today?"

"As a matter of fact I will. But, I have back-to-back appointments. How 'bout we meet for lunch rather than you coming by my office?"

"I'd like that."

"Say, the country club, at noon?"

"Sounds wonderful. I'll see you there, at noon."

Caroline hung up the phone and began to plan her day. She brightened having something to look forward to. As she brushed her hair, she wondered how much she should tell Paul. *I don't want him to think I'm going off the deep end. He'd have me committed or, worse yet, tell The Senator!*

Caroline suddenly stopped brushing. *What was that?* She listened intently for the noise to repeat itself. It sounded like a cabinet drawer being slammed shut in the kitchen. After listening for a while, nothing else had happened, so she shook her head and began her morning facial regimen. *Probably the timbers creaking or something from outside. But still...* The hair at the nape of her neck rose, as panic started to set in. After all, she was alone in this great big house. It took a stern self-talk to get her heart rate steady, again. The shower refreshed her, and she felt better as the effects of the sleeping pills wore off.

It felt good to be back in familiar surroundings. Strange settings still unnerved her. Looking through her closet, she finally selected her old standbys, a white chiffon long sleeved blouse and black slacks. With a closet full of fine clothes, she always seemed to pick the same ones.

As Caroline was applying her makeup, she heard the strange noise, again. She froze. Together, with the events of the previous evening, the mysterious noise was just too much. She had to get out of there. She grabbed her jacket and handbag and ran down the stairs and into the garage. As she punched the garage door open, she fumbled in her purse for the keys to her Thunderbird. *Damn, where are they?* Then, it hit her. They were in the drawer in the kitchen. That's where she and Grant traditionally kept the keys to both vehicles because neither could remember where they had last put them. Grant always used the Lincoln. Caroline preferred the Thunderbird, a gift from The Senator upon her graduation from college. Caroline turned and stared at the entrance back into the house. The haunted house. She was sure of it, and now she had to go back into it. Resolutely, she took a step and then another.

Peering into the kitchen, she checked for apparitions, or at least a burglar. She almost preferred a burglar, when she thought of it. Seeing neither, she slowly walked to the drawer and opened it. The keys were not there. She looked in the other drawers, shoving their contents around roughly. They were nowhere to be found. *Please don't tell me they're upstairs!* All she wanted to do was get the hell out of there!

Caroline hesitated. At some moment on this strange search, a niggling had begun. She felt a strong pull towards the drawing room, just like last night. Her feet moved while her mind rebelled, and before she knew it, she was standing at the room's doorway. She noticed the mess she had made with the sheet music, but skimmed by it without hesitation. When she reached the piano, she righted the bench and slid onto it like it was a familiar throne. Of their own volition, her hands raised the piano cover. They hovered over the keys for a moment and then began playing. The song was one of her favorites. Grant occasionally bestowed it on her when he wanted to please her, or to request a favor. She was unable to stop her fingers, unable to lift her hands from the keys.

When at last the melody ended, Caroline rose, now in a trance-like state, and went to her bedroom. She slumped onto her bed and was instantly asleep.

Caroline, my love, you played that beautifully. Together we make a great team. Just wait, my darling, when you audition with the symphony, they won't believe their ears.

TWO HOURS later, Caroline was startled awake by the ringing of the phone. It was

Paul. "Caroline, I've been worried sick about you. I waited for over an hour, but you didn't show up. I've cancelled my appointments and I'm coming over."

"Oh, my God! I'm so sorry." Confused at first, Caroline sat up and looked around. Then realizing she was in her bedroom, she remembered what had happened. She stammered, "I went to rest for a few minutes and must have dozed off. Please forgive me. There is no need to come over. I'm all right."

"I've already made arrangements for my receptionist to cancel my appointments. Let me come by, just for my own peace of mind. The Senator would never forgive me if anything happened to you."

Caroline thought fast. She certainly didn't want Paul to come over, but under no circumstances did she want her father involved, at least not at this juncture. She could see it was either Paul or her father, and the choice was clear. "Since you put it that way, I'll be expecting you."

"I'm on my way," Paul said.

After giving her cell phone an irritated look, Caroline went back to the drawing room. No goose bumps presented themselves, so she went in. She sat down at the piano and touched the keys in a haphazard fashion, but was unable to play anything that sounded remotely like music. She was, however, certain now that Grant—that is his spirit—she corrected herself, *had* talked to her, the night before. She tried to dredge up his words from her subconscious. There was something about her having received more than his blood in the transfusion. She tried, but couldn't remember anything else. For now, he wasn't playing the piano through her. Apparently, she could play only at his direction.

Caroline pondered the dilemma for a few minutes, and then closed the cover over the keyboard, picked up the scattered sheet music, and straightened the room. She went to the kitchen to brew her favorite coffee from the freshly ground coffee beans she purchased from Starbuck's. The aroma of the coffee brewing jostled memories of bringing coffee to their bedroom to watch the news together, before starting their separate days. Remembering curling up next to her husband, wrapped in his embrace, caused tears to well in her eyes. Caroline shook herself free from the reverie and went to the freezer. She perused the assortment of cookies and baked goods. The couple had kept a supply on hand, as they often had friends drop in, unexpectedly. Caroline was busy arranging pecan cookies on a crystal platter when the doorbell rang. She hurried to the front door and, opening it, greeted Paul with a warm embrace.

"Paul, thank you for your concern but, really, there was no need."

"I wanted to see for myself that you're doing well. You look rested. Perhaps the nap was more important than lunch with an old man."

"Nonsense! You're not an old man. What's that mantra you're always spewing to your older patients; 'Age is a number, not a condition'?"

"Drat! Snared in my own trap."

"I just brewed a fresh pot of coffee. Want a cup?"

"You bet. Smells good. I'll just go into the drawing—"

"No!" Caroline didn't know what to expect from Grant, so she steered Paul away. "Come into the kitchen. I put out some cookies for you. Your favorites, of course."

Caroline busied herself, all the while trying to get control of her shaking hands. With her back facing Paul, she said, "I didn't mean to come across so harshly. It's just that Grant was so adamant about eating and drinking in that room. It was just a knee-jerk reaction. Of course, if you want, we can have our coffee, in there."

"You know what, out of respect for Grant, I'd rather not. Let's stay in here; it's warmer and friendlier."

"As you wish." Caroline released a quiet sigh.

Sitting at the counter stirring sugar into his coffee, Paul said, "I've known you since you were a baby, Caroline. Something is bothering you. Granted, you have gone through a lot."

"Don't worry, Paul. I really am doing well. As a matter of fact, today is the first time since the accident that I am able to say that." She laughed lightly. "That's good, isn't it?"

"Well, yes. But, something just isn't clicking. You seem…different."

"In what way?" Caroline was apprehensive. *Surely, he couldn't guess that Grant was here?*

"That's the mystery. I can't quite put my finger on it, but it's there."

"Come on, Paul. I've only been home one day. I'm just getting oriented and trying to put my life together. You're making something out of nothing."

"Think so? I'm not so sure. Why don't we make an appointment for next week for you to come in for a good once over? Give me a chance to use my medical skills."

"If you insist, but you're wasting your time. I assure you I'm just fine."

"Humor me! Call my office and make the appointment. Otherwise, I'm calling The Senator."

"Oh, no. Not that!" Caroline laughed. "However, I expect to see him on my doorstep, any day now, so don't waste your dime calling him."

"Be kind. You know, after your mother died, your father was devastated. You became his whole world. I dread to think what would happen to him, if anything also befell you. You should have seen him the entire time you were recovering. I thought we were going to have another patient on our hands."

"I know." *When was I ever part of The Senator's world, much less his whole world?* "I love him dearly for all that he is, but I barely remember him from my childhood and especially after he went into politics. All I learned was mostly from newspaper articles and Nettie. You remember, my nanny? I don't know much about the years he was a United States senator.

Mother died shortly after he was elected and, a few years later, I was sent away to school."

"Your father sent you to the best schools knowing you would need a good education to make it in today's world. I doubt there is a day that goes by that he doesn't mention you. Never doubt he loves you with all his heart."

"If you say so," Caroline whispered. *Maybe he mentioned me daily, but he didn't bother to contact me. He may have called every other month, but that was only out of a sense of duty.*

"There is something I would like to ask you, Paul." She refilled his coffee cup. "Do you know much about, um, about the afterlife?"

"HA! What does anyone know about the afterlife? I do believe in Jesus' teachings. My childhood years as a Catholic left a deep impression on me. Other than what we learn from our religion, I'm as much in the dark, as anyone."

"Do you think, er, mediums can really contact the other side?"

"Come on, Caroline. Are you suggesting that you want to try to contact Grant? I think it's all hocus-pocus. Don't waste your money."

Sensing Paul was getting suspicious, Caroline said, "I suppose you're right. It was just a thought triggered by, ah, by some TV program I was watching, late one night. At the hospital."

"That so? Anyway, promise me you're not going to pursue this nonsense any further."

"Now would I do that?" Caroline skirted around making a direct promise she suspected she was going to have to break.

"I would hope not. It's not healthy for you to be thinking about something like that. You know in your soul that such a thing is not possible," Paul said, glancing at the wall clock in the kitchen. "I should go. Oh, by the way, I noticed your garage door was open when I drove up. Were you going somewhere?"

Good gosh, I forgot I opened the garage before coming in for the car keys. "No. I was, ah, letting in some fresh air. You know the house has been closed up for three months. I opened the garage door because I thought some fresh air would clear out the musty smell. When you showed up, I completely forgot about it. Which reminds me, did I ever thank you for engaging the housekeeper to clean before I came home? If not, I'm doing so, now."

"You're welcome." Paul rose from his chair. "Well, kiddo, the sick and suffering await my healing powers, so I will bid you ado. However, I must insist you call for an appointment—no negotiating on that point. Do I make myself clear?"

Caroline remained silent. Spending more time with a doctor, even an old family friend, almost made her physically ill. She put her arm through his, as they approached the door, where he planted the traditional kiss on her forehead before exiting the residence.

"Thanks for coming by. I really do appreciate your care and concern. You're a dear."

Paul, already in the driveway, turned and waved acknowledgement before he squeezed his six foot two frame into the Lexus. Caroline, with a sense of relief, watched him drive away.

CHAPTER

3

I hate like hell having to lie to Paul. Caroline went into her study and turned on her computer. She wanted to learn more about psychic phenomenon. She pulled up the names of several psychics in the New Orleans area. One medium had posted a video of a reading, so she watched to get an idea of how readings were conducted. This particular session was one-on-one, as opposed to a group reading. She surmised the groups were probably tantamount to séances.

Caroline watched as the medium sat down facing the client, who was obviously very nervous. The medium asked, "What is it you're seeking?"

Having been prompted, the client began, "I, ah, er, okay, why do the departed make themselves known?"

"They come through because, well simply, because that is their method of communication."

"You say they 'come through.' What is the method they use to do so?"

"Spirits can channel through anyone. Once a person is trained to recognize their presence, they can even channel through you."

"Is that so? From what I understand from reading your books, you contend my deceased relatives: my mother, father, ah, sister...are all still here?"

"Absolutely, that is what I'm saying."

"I mean *here*. Present with us, *here* in this room."

"Yes."

"I'm—I don't know what to say."

"Let me help you. Do you have a close relative still living?"

"Yes."

"How close? Sibling, cousin...?"

"I have a brother, in California."

The medium paused and cocked his head to one side.

"I'm getting Ray. Is his name Ray?"

The stunned client stared at the medium. Noting the look on the client's face, the medium continued, "Your mother is telling me that Ray walks with a limp. He broke his leg as a child, and it wasn't set properly."

"Yes! We were playing in the orchard! Uh, Mother told you that?"

"Yes. She also wants you to know that she is with your father and sister, and they are happy where they are."

The client fainted.

CAROLINE WROTE down the medium's telephone number and switched off the computer. She was desperate for answers so she dialed the number to see if maybe she could schedule an appointment.

"Good afternoon. This is Quinton Lucas' answering service. How may I direct your call?" the representative asked.

"Yes, good afternoon. I'm calling for an appointment with Quinton Lucas."

"I will put you through to his office. He may not answer if he is with a client, but you can leave a message."

"Thank you."

The phone rang once, and a pleasant male voice answered, "This is Quinton Lucas. To whom am I speaking?"

"Hello, Mr. Lucas. I'm calling for an appointment for a reading. I'd like to see you as soon as possible."

"Sounds serious. I have this evening open. I schedule two hour sessions. Have I seen you before?"

"Ah, no, you haven't. What time is this evening's appointment?"

"Seven to nine. May I have your name and contact information?"

"Ah, my name is… Jenn, Jennifer Marking."

"Well, *Jennifer*, I detect a lot of anxiety in your voice, perhaps we can put your mind at ease." Then after a pause, he said, "If you want the appointment, I'll see you at seven?"

"Yes, yes, I definitely want the appointment. I'll be there. Thank you."

AFTER HANGING up the phone, Caroline launched a search for the missing car keys. Being unsuccessful in her efforts, she finally went back to her starting place, the kitchen, and stood at the counter pondering where the keys might be. Just to satisfy her curiosity, she opened the drawer where the keys were usually kept. They were there, lying right on top of the telephone book! *How could I have missed them before?* She picked them up and gaped at the very thought they were in her hand. *Curiouser and curiouser.*

Caroline put the keys in her pocket, where they'd be safe until she needed them later that evening. She spent the rest of the afternoon doing domestic chores. While folding her freshly-dried laundry she reflected on the way the medium said *Jennifer*, after she gave him the name. Had he detected her deception? If so, she was impressed. She was also relieved in being able to get an appointment so quickly. *I can't*

*go through another night of Grant's visitations without
knowing for sure if it's him, or if I'm crazier than I think.
If Mr. Lucas could detect my lie over the phone, he must
be the real deal.*

AT PRECISELY 6:15, Caroline left her
home and drove to the French Quarter. The psychic
was located close to a famous New Orleans hotel,
The Inn on Bourbon. During the years she attended
Tulane, she and her friends explored New Orleans quite thoroughly and especially the French
Quarter. Caroline knew the area well, so she pulled
into a parking garage close to her destination, Rue
Chartres Street. Although *Mardi Gras* had come
and gone, the French Quarter was still teaming
with activity, and it appeared to Caroline that the
partygoers were perpetually alive and well.

Bourbon Street was lined with shops which
stayed open late into the night. Neon signs illuminated the sidewalk, and music filled the air. Caroline looked up and smiled when she saw strands of
the traditional *Mardi Gras* purple, gold, and green
beads hanging from the electric wires high above.
During the parade, it was customary to stand on
hotel balconies and toss beads to those below.
Apparently, some of the beads were flung a bit high
and were stranded on the wires.

The French Quarter had always fascinated
Caroline. As she left the parking garage, she walked

past a small shop that featured voodoo parapher-
nalia in the window. From the time she enrolled
in Tulane, Caroline had heard stories—some no
doubt true—regarding the infamous Voodoo
Queen, Marie Laveau. The display in the shop
window was centered on Laveau's potions and talis-
manic charms. Of all the stories associated with the
mystery and charm of New Orleans, Marie Laveau
was the one that intrigued Caroline the most.

Peering at the display, Caroline remembered
the local icon was born in the late 1700s. She was
renowned as a *Loahs*, or of voodoo deity. Legend
had it that her voodoo skills could help you "get
a lover, keep a lover, or get rid of a lover" with her
special array of potions and magic. It was common
knowledge that people still visited her gravesite to
request favors. The tradition is to leave her gifts of
money, cigars, white rum, or candy as payment for
the requested favor. Caroline, herself, was seeking a
miracle, but from a different source—one, however,
that offered the same intrigue.

Caroline checked her watch, and then verified
the address she had scribbled on the scrap of paper
she'd retrieved from her shoulder bag. She surveyed
her surroundings. She recalled being in the curio
shop that was directly across the street. She had
been there several times to purchase souvenirs for
friends and a supply of beads to fling from the
balcony during the parade. Two doors up the street
was a small quaint bar. Loud music emptied out into
the bustling boulevard. Caroline felt comfortable in

the midst of the hustle and bustle. She honed in on the address she was seeking and crammed the scrap of paper back into her shoulder bag. Just as she stepped off the curb, a swarm of partygoers passed and swept her up, entreating her to join them. It seemed like every day in the French Quarter was a mini-Mardi Gras.

"Come on, baby, lighten up," one enthusiastic, very intoxicated male called to her, over the din of his squealing and laughing comrades. He held out his drink, offering to share it with her.

Caroline laughed and held up her hands in mock protest. Pulling free from the crowd, she said, "Not now, but thanks, anyway. I'm on a different mission." She continued across the street, hurrying toward the medium's office building.

A clock somewhere near chimed seven times, just as Caroline entered the suite of Quinton Lucas. The waiting area was friendly, warm, and comfortable. Caroline looked around for a buzzer or some other way to let Mr. Lucas know she was there. Nothing. She took a seat, smoothing her slacks and crossing her ankles in a ladylike position. She wanted to make a good impression.

She had just come to the conclusion this was a waste of time, when the wooden and glass door on the opposite end of the room swung open. A handsome, thirties-something man appeared, strode over to Caroline, and extended his hand.

"Good evening, *Jennifer*. I'm Quinton Lucas."

"Pleased to meet you, Mr. Lucas." Caroline took in his tall and rugged frame, but her gaze stumbled when she encountered the bluest eyes she had ever seen. They seemed to probe her soul, yet with a kind and gentle touch. Add it all up, and Quinton Lucas was not at all what she'd expected in a psychic.

"Come into my office," he said, gesturing toward the open door. "Would you like a soft drink or some water?"

"Ah, yes, some water would be welcome. My mouth is suddenly very dry."

"I get that a lot. Have a seat, I'll be right back."

Quinton Lucas left the room, and Caroline was grateful for time to gather herself. She actually found that she was attracted to this stranger, but wasn't sure how far to trust him. After all, psychic mediums were a new concept to her, and he could very well be a shyster, for all she knew. It was those eyes! She wondered if all his clients were mesmerized by them. *I bet he could tell them anything, and they'd believe him, all because of those eyes.* She determined that they wouldn't fool her. A few minutes later, the psychic reappeared with a bottle of water in each hand. He twisted the cap off of one and offered it to Caroline.

"Thank you, Mr. Lucas."

"Call me Luke. I like to be on a first name basis with my clients. May I call you Jenn?"

"What? Oh, yes, of course."

"Okay, Jenn, it is. We're on the clock. What is it that's bothering you?"

Caroline looked down at her hands, which were folded in her lap. "Well, I don't know where to begin. Everything seems surreal, and now I'm feeling foolish for coming here."

"Why don't we have an informal chat, for starters?" Luke said. "Did you grow up in New Orleans?"

"No, I was raised in Charleston. I attended Tulane after high school. That's where I met and eventually married my late husband."

"I see. Has this something to do with your late husband? What's holding you back? You don't have to reveal your true identity." He held up his hand at Caroline's protest. "But you should know, everything that transpires between us is confidential. I suspect Jennifer isn't your real name but, if you prefer, I'll play along. I don't know how much I can help you, though, if you won't open up completely to me.

"And, just to let you know, while you were waiting for me, I got a transmission from someone named Garth or Grant. I sensed he had a message for you. However, he vanished before telling me what it was."

Caroline gasped. "Are you sure?"

"Yes, I'm sure. That's my business."

"My husband's name was Grant. He's been appearing in my dreams ever since I arrived home from the hospital, two days ago."

"Now, we're getting somewhere. Tell me what happened."

"I'm embarrassed." Caroline felt her cheeks get hot and took a swig of water. "I should have known I couldn't keep up the charade much longer. My real name is Caroline Alexander. I was married to Grant Alexander. He was killed about three months ago in a terrible automobile accident. I was with him, but I survived. We were returning home from a symphony. He is, er, *was* a concert pianist."

Caroline was encouraged that Luke sat silent, but attentive, during her monologue. There was no cynicism in those blue eyes. *Good. Maybe I'm not so crazy after all.* She found the courage to continue her story, including how the doctors saved her life with the blood transfusion between Grant and herself, and of spending three months in the hospital recovering.

She paused and studied Luke's reaction. He tilted his head and smiled for her to go on. She shrugged.

"That's all?" Luke asked, "Grant didn't contact you in the hospital, did he?"

"No. Not that I'm aware of. I was sedated, almost unconscious, most of the time. I had reconstructive surgery and was in a lot of pain. I don't remember many details about the time in the hospital. It all started the day I came home. That was yesterday. An old family friend, Paul Bruno, brought me home. After Paul left, an unexplainable sensation forced me into the drawing room. It was then that

I experienced an uncontrollable urge to play the piano. I felt as though I was in a trance and had no control, as I sat down at the piano and began to play. The piece was the solo concerto Grant played the night he died. I played it expertly. I had never seriously played the piano before, nor had I ever had the desire to do so. The fact is, a kitten on the keys can play better than I.

"When I finished playing, I was so frightened that I jumped up, scattering sheet music everywhere. I ran to our, er, my bedroom and locked the door. I have a prescription sedative to help me sleep, so I took some—probably too many—and lay down and was soon fast asleep. In my sleep, I remember feeling Grant's presence. I thought that was the first visit I had from Grant until I eventually realized it was him making me play the piano. So, his talking to me in my sleep must have been the second visit. He told me about how he was going to make me a world renowned pianist by him playing through me. When I awoke, I thought it was all just a dream until I went downstairs and saw the music all over the floor.

"I felt I had to get out of the house. I'd been hospitalized for so long, and the unsettling events upon my homecoming had me on edge, so I called Paul, and we scheduled lunch. After getting ready, I went to the garage and I discovered I didn't have my car keys. I went back into the house to get them. Almost immediately, I found myself in the same weird trance. Some force directed me to the drawing room, and I sat down and began playing the piano, again."

Caroline paused long enough to take a drink from the water bottle. She then continued: "When I finished, much like the night before, I went to my room and fell into a deep sleep. I don't remember how long I slept, but the phone woke me up. It was Paul. He was almost frantic because I hadn't shown up for our luncheon date, and he wanted to know why I stood him up." Caroline nervously toyed with the water bottle. "I couldn't tell him about what I suspected were Grant's visits. He would have had me committed." She paused. "Do you think you can help me?"

Luke looked directly into her green eyes and said, "Yes, I do think I can help you. I've read books on how a recipient of a transplant may take on some of the characteristics of the donor. Although it may appear unusual, it really isn't. Conclusive studies reveal that all living cells retain a memory and decider subsystems—"

"Whoa, wait up. You're getting way ahead of me. What are decider subsystems?"

"Ah, thank you for stopping me. I get carried away when I talk shop. Not to be too technical, in answer to your question, the decider is the executive subsystem which receives input from all other subsystems and transmits that information to the entire system.

"My research also shows that it is proven that all dynamical systems store information and energy in various degrees. One of the studies I explored reports that sensitive recipients may experience some of the donor's history, which is stored in the transplanted cells. This now brings us back to your dilemma, Caroline. Quite simply, the transplanted cells may give the recipient a *legacy*, an inheritance, so to speak, of the donor's characteristics, such as talent."

"Oh, my God…" Caroline murmured. "You mean I'm stuck with Grant's whatchama-call-it systems?"

Luke grinned. "Well, I don't know about stuck. It's too early to make that determination. I recall one study wherein the recipient had a sudden craving for fast food burgers. She had been a health fanatic and wouldn't go near fast food before the transplant. Afterwards, she craved greasy burgers. She likened it to an uncontrollable urge—much like what you describe with reference to your piano playing. I can tell this interests you?"

"Yes, very much so. I'm frantic for answers."

"And, I'm eager to supply them." Luke continued, "Another study revealed that the recipient of a heart transplant suddenly was able to play music, never having done so before. Again, much like what you've described to me. I recall several of the studies related to the recipients playing musical instruments of one sort or another. So your situation isn't that far off the chart.

"Transplants can transfer to the recipient more than talent. Another case I found in the literature tells of a young man who received the heart of a middle-aged woman. He claims he went on to become one of the world's greatest lovers. Of course, that's a metaphor. But, facts disclosed that after his recovery, he looked at women differently, in a more sensitive and sensual manner.

"These are just a few examples of actual cases. I'll refer you to the book that details case-after-case accounts regarding this phenomenon. You can take comfort in knowing your situation is not unique."

"I should think these events would be news-worthy. How is it that I've never heard of them before?" Caroline asked.

"Well, you know how it goes. If it isn't bad news…"

"I guess so, however, I am relieved to know I'm not alone in this realm. You've answered some of my concerns. What about the dreams? Did the partic-ipants in the studies talk about having dreams, like I do?"

"Not the ones I researched, but that doesn't mean they didn't." Luke put his elbows on the desk and tented his fingers while he studied Caroline. "Why don't we test the waters? We can begin by trying to communicate with Grant, directly. It may take a few visits but, believe me, there is a solution. My question to you now is, are you ready to accept whatever we uncover?"

Caroline shuddered. "That gives me the chills. What I'm hearing is I may have inherited Grant's talent through the transfusion. In plain English, is that what you're telling me?"

"Stated quite simply, yes, you're correct."

"Is this going to be bad?"

"No, not necessarily. The people in the studies with which I'm familiar seem to be happy with their newly conferred abilities. How bad can it be to suddenly become a wonderful and talented pianist?"

"I suppose you have a point, there," Caroline snapped, "but, that's not what I want to do with my life. And, I dread going to sleep knowing Grant, in all likelihood, will make his presence known, in some form or another. I don't think I can tolerate this situation, much longer. It's scary and—and creepy. I'm beginning to think I'm going off the deep end, if I've not already done so. If I agree to his suggestion, will I ever be free of him? Don't misunderstand me; I loved Grant with all my heart. I was content just being a wife, his wife."

"Easy, Caroline, quell those crazy thoughts. You're not losing your mind. We will get to the bottom of this, and you will have peace. Initially, I believe Grant has a message for you. We need to find out what it is, then proceed from there."

"I know what it is. He told me in a dream. He wants to continue to play, using me as a conduit. His exact words were: 'Together, we will set the world on fire.' Now that he's dead, I don't want to be trapped with him, in that state. How would you feel knowing you had a dead person inside you, controlling you and your life?"

Luke was very still. "I've never had a case quite like this one. Your story is unique due to the accompanying dreams. This is a new phenomenon for me. It's intriguing, and I'm anxious to get answers, not just for you, but for myself, as well." He went to where Caroline sat, moved a chair next to hers, and took her hand in his.

"I'm going to try to contact Grant. He may not feel comfortable revealing himself, since I'm here with you. It may take a few visits to convince him I'm a friend. If, however, we are able to connect, let him do the talking. From what you've told me, it appears he is eager to establish a link from beyond. We will be able to assess the situation more when the session ends."

"I'm okay with that," Caroline responded in a weak, shaky voice.

"Okay, let's get start—"

"NO!" Caroline gripped his arm like it was a life preserver. "Wait, I'm not ready. I don't know if I can do this. I—I—the experiences of the last two days have left me drained and—and to be frank, I'm scared. I don't know anything about contacting the other side, and it—it—"

"There is nothing to fear. The spirits will not harm you. I will be in control. Grant will use me to relay his message, when he's ready. He will not physically manifest himself."

"But, what if he continues to visit me in my dreams? I can't deal with it. I'm pretty fragile after the accident and almost dying myself! I'm having second thoughts about doing this. Maybe we ought to wait."

Luke nodded. "Why don't we quit, for now, and give you a chance to absorb what you've learned this evening?" Luke rounded his desk and scribbled on a note pad. "I suggest you pick up this book and read it before our next session," he said, as he tore the note from the pad and handed it to Caroline.

"Next session? I'm not sure…"

"Of course. At any rate, I urge you to read the book. Come, I'll see you out. I'm ready to leave and need to lock up. Since we didn't use your full two hours, I'll walk you to your car."

Caroline looked at her watch. "It's almost nine. I've been here almost two hours?"

Luke leaned over and looked at her watch, remarking, "Yes, ma'am, Seikos don't lie." Luke turned and surveyed his suite. "Seems everything's in order. Are you ready to go?"

Caroline nodded.

Luke ushered Caroline out the door, and then locked it behind them.

"Where did you park?" he asked.

"In the parking garage in the next block. I appreciate the escort. I am rather ragged from everything that has been happening, lately. All I need is another scare, and I'll surely go over the edge."

Luke laughed. "You're not even close to the abyss."

THE STREETS of the French Quarter were teaming with revelers, many of whom had too much to drink, several drinks ago. The atmosphere was light and gay, as couples and groups strolled along laughing and singing.

Caroline and Luke passed a mime that was poised in the middle of the block. Caroline wondered if he was real or a painted sculpture. Passersby would make faces at him and even resort to ridiculous antics, but the mime stood unflappable.

The couple walked past two raggedy young lads, tap dancing under a street lamp. As they passed, one of the boys pointed to the tin cup they had strategically placed at their feet. Luke smiled, as he reached into his pants pocket and tossed a handful of change into the cup.

When Caroline and Luke turned the corner, making their way to the parking garage, they walked by a small café in the middle of the block. Peeking over his shoulder, Luke asked, "Would you like something to eat or drink? *Daisy's* is one of my favorites."

"You must have heard my stomach growl. Suddenly, I'm ravenous." Caroline looked back at the café. "I've been to *Daisy's*, in fact, many times. I would come here with some of my sorority sisters after a night on the town, back in my college days.

They serve the most delightful Lost Bread I've ever eaten. Would you share some with me?"

"I'd be happy to share, but you're welcome to have your own order."

"Clearly, you haven't had Lost Bread, there. It's *Daisy's* version of French toast. The servings are enough for two large men. I always order it because it's so delicious, but then I end up leaving more than half."

"Okay—you got yourself a deal," Luke said, as the two walked back. Luke held the door open for Caroline.

Luke requested a table by a window, so they could watch the night life. Once they were seated, and the waitress took their order, Luke said, "You mentioned you grew up in Charleston. What was that like?"

"I love Charleston. The city is, well, electric. It's exciting, albeit nothing like New Orleans. The people are southern friendly, although some can be snobs—you know, the privileged Daughters of the Revolution syndrome."

"Indeed I do. We have some of those, here."

"I've noticed," Caroline commented taking a sip from her water glass. "My father, Winston Schumann, was a four-term senator. He is now retired and lives in the family home in the heart of all of that Civil War history. Mother died when I was four. I have only vague memories of her. The Senator, as required by his position, was in DC for most of my childhood. I was raised by a loving nursemaid."

"Come to think of it, you do resemble Scarlett." Luke studied her.

"Now, don't you start! Grant always teased me about Scarlett. In fact, my wedding dress was very similar to the dress Scarlett wore at the famous picnic at Twelve Oaks, before the start of the war and…" Caroline sighed.

"And, what?"

"Oh, it's just that Grant was enamored by *Gone With the Wind*. Sometimes I think that may be why he married me—because I resembled Scarlett," Caroline said, toying with the lime wedge perched on the edge of her water glass.

"Don't stop! I want to hear more. Please continue."

At that moment, the waitress reappeared with their order and two dinner plates. After the waitress departed, Luke placed an equal share on each plate. "I see what you mean," he said. "There *is* enough for two Saints linebackers, and maybe the whole line."

Taking her knife and fork in hand, Caroline said, "Let me show you how I indulge in the sheer rapture of an overdose of Lost Bread." She smiled, as she placed a pat of butter on her steaming portion. "First you slather butter on all the exposed areas." She then took the pitcher of warm maple syrup from the carousel. "Then you drown it in syrup. Pure heaven!" Audibly groaning, she raised the first titillating bite to her lips.

"Hey, wait for me," Luke retorted. Mimicking Caroline, he smeared butter and sloshed syrup lavishly on his portion.

"There is no waiting in Lost Bread consumption," Caroline said, as she shoveled in the tasty morsels in quick spurts. "Bet I beat you."

"Sure, since you got a head start," Luke replied, as syrup dripped from his fork onto his tie. He looked down and smiled in naughty boy fashion. He took his napkin, dipped it into his water glass, and dabbed at the spot.

Caroline seemed oblivious to Luke's predicament. When she crammed the last bite into her mouth, she squealed, "Ta Da!" She threw her hands up imitating the universal signal for touchdown. "I win. But, you get extra points for being such a good sport." She grinned, as she watched Luke stuff a huge bite into his mouth.

"Ha! You call that finished? Look at the crumbs and puddles of syrup languishing there," Luke croaked through a full mouth. "It's not over 'til it's over. What was that wager, again? Did I hear you say if you lost, you would have dinner with me, tomorrow night, and if I lost, I would have dinner with you, tomorrow night?"

"Your memory is faulty—I don't remember saying anything of the kind. Sounds more like heads you win, tails I lose."

"HO, HO! Not only are you a cheater and a glutton, you also renege on your bets."

"You're impossible, but just to keep you from ruining my reputation, I accept."

Luke smiled and looked out of the window as a group of exceptionally loud partygoers caroused by the café. A voluptuous blond diva, obviously very intoxicated, waved at Luke. He waved back. She held up her drink in salute and motioned with her free hand for him to join the party. Luke shook his head and then reached for his wallet. Looking at the dinner check, he extracted a twenty and placed it on the tray with the check. He stood and offered his arm to Caroline. "Let's go. I better get you to that car of yours."

As they approached Caroline's T-bird, she handed Luke the keys. He unlocked the driver's door and held it for her, as she gracefully slid onto the leather seat. When she was situated, he said, "I'll pick you up at seven, tomorrow evening. Dress casual and wear comfortable shoes. After dinner, we're going to do some sight-seeing."

"Now you've piqued my interest. Where are we going?"

"You'll see. Don't you like surprises?"

"I love surprises—if they're of the good variety. I've had all of the bad ones I can handle, for a while."

"Then you'll love this one. Drive safely, see you tomorrow."

"But, you don't know where I live!"

"You're forgetting who you're talking to. I *will* find you." Luke smiled and closed her car door.

Then, he stepped back and motioned for her to exit. He saluted Caroline, as she started to drive away. Suddenly, she stopped and backed up. From the window, she yelled, "I haven't paid you for your services."

"I'll take an IOU, and you can pay me, later."

"You're awfully trusting," Caroline called out the window, as she drove away.

CHAPTER

4

The next evening Luke rang Caroline's doorbell, as the clock in the foyer chimed seven times. "Now, that's what I call punctual," Caroline said, as she opened the door. She was dressed in black slacks, light green short sleeved T-shirt, and black Nike's. The T-shirt emphasized more than her green eyes.

"I've learned to be on time. If I miss a beat, I'm behind the entire day. You look very posh. What happened to casual?"

Caroline looked down at her attire, and said, "This is casual."

"Guess we come from opposite sides of the tracks," Luke said, looking down at his loose fitting jeans, over-sized Saints T-shirt, and boots. He glanced up and his eyes met hers. He asked, "If you don't mind, I would like to look around the house to get a sense of your surroundings. It could be helpful for future sessions."

"Of course. Come in."

"Where is this infamous piano?" he asked, entering the foyer.

"It's over there," Caroline remarked, pointing to the drawing room. "Are you already on to something?"

"Yes. I'm feeling some energy, but the source is somewhat obscure. Do you feel like playing?"

Luke noticed the confused look on Caroline's face, so he quickly added. "The piano, I mean."

"Oh, no! Not now, anyway. I cannot play unless Grant is directing me—and I have no control over when he does so."

Luke nodded. He circled the piano being careful not to touch it. "I don't want to interfere with the energy I'm feeling, so I won't touch the piano. It seems to be a catalyst." Caroline watched him with interest, and after a few moments, he asked, "May I see the rest of the house?"

"Why, yes," Caroline responded, and led Luke through adjacent rooms.

When they entered the master suite, he asked, "Is this where you experience the dreams?"

"Yes. Why? Is that important?"

"I'm just getting a feel for the surroundings, so I can accurately interpret Grant's intervention. By the way, I forgot to ask, did you have a dream last night, after meeting with me?"

"No, although I expected to have one, it didn't happen. Why do you think it didn't?   "

"I'm not sure, just yet. Remember, this is fairly new territory for me, as well."

"I'm a wreck. You do believe me, don't you?"

"Yes, I believe you." Surveying the room, Luke said, "I think we can leave, now. I've seen all I need to. Bring a jacket. It may cool off, later in the evening."

THE COUPLE sat in silence on the drive to the French Quarter. Luke parked in his reserved parking space close to his office. "I know a restaurant that specializes in southern soul and Cajun Creole. How does that sound?"

"Wonderful. Two of my favorites, soul and Creole. It's possible I may have been there during my college rampages. What's the name of the restaurant?"

"*Marte's.*"

"Of course, I should have guessed. I have been there several times. It's close to one of my favorite curio shops."

"So, you approve?"

"Absolutely!"

"Since you're so well-traveled, have you been to *The Cotton Club*?"

"I've heard of it, but have never been there. It looked pretty rough for sorority girls."

"No argument there. It has a pretty crude atmosphere. There's no bar, no air or heat, and rough benches to sit on, that is, if you're lucky enough to get a seat. Don't let the looks fool you. The music is sensational. The band is composed of a group of veteran musicians organized to keep traditional jazz alive. If you like jazz, you'll be impressed. Although the building is a dump, people stand in line for hours just to get inside. It's been on-going for over forty years. It's just a short walk from here. We could stop by there after dinner, if you're game."

"I think that sounds like an adventure and, of course, I'm game. Who wouldn't be?"

WHEN LUKE and Caroline finally gained admission into *The Cotton Club*, they had to snake their way through the throng of patrons waiting for a chance encounter with the musicians.

"Who knew?" Caroline shouted to Luke, as they stood with the crowd, listening to an array of musicians playing jazz. Caroline was caught in the moment, enjoying the atmosphere as much as the music.

"This is fantastic. I love jazz," Caroline said, swaying to the beat and mingling with the crowd.

"I thought you might. This has been one of my favorite haunts since I first came to New Orleans. It is a good place to forget one's problems. Caroline, is something wrong?"

Suddenly, without warning, Caroline began to push her way through the crowd.

"Hey, wait up. Where are you...what are you doing?" Luke called, as he elbowed his way through the crowd, trying to catch Caroline. She approached the bandstand, and was met by the lead musician, who smiled at her. She asked him something, and he nodded. Within moments, she was seated at the weathered upright piano, waiting for her cue from the band leader. Caroline played a medley of southern favorites, accompanied by the band. When they concluded with a rendition of "When the Saints Go Marching In," the crowd went wild. They clapped and howled their approval. At the conclusion of her performance, Caroline rose, bowed, and left the bandstand.

Halfway back to Luke, she stumbled, a look of sheer terror on her face. Luke rushed to her side.

"Did he...? Was that him?"

Caroline clung to Luke, on the verge of tears. "Yes. Luke, I found myself compelled to that bandstand! There was nothing I could do." She felt tears slide down her cheeks. "I hope there's something you can do to help me. I'm terrified!"

"Let's get out of here." Luke said, leading her through the heavy throng and holding her close, as they exited. She was near collapse by the time they hit the night air. She held Luke's arm tightly, and sobbed, "It's hopeless! No matter what we do, Grant *will* have his way."

As they passed *Daisy's*, Luke said, "The place looks pretty empty. Let's go in, so you can sit for a while. I could use another round of Lost Bread, if you're up to it."

Caroline managed to smile, but tears still brimmed and threatened to overflow. "Thanks for the offer, but if you don't mind, I would rather just go home."

"Sure. That's probably a better idea."

UPON ARRIVAL at the Alexander's mansion, Luke pulled into the driveway. "Come on, I'll walk you in."

"NO! Wait," Caroline groaned. "I'm not sure I want to go in. This whole ordeal has been frightening, and I…I don't want to stay here, alone. At least, not tonight."

Luke scratched his head "I have a spare room."

"Are you sure you don't mind? I don't want to impose."

"Not at all." Luke put the car in reverse and backed out of the driveway.

LUKE RESIDED in the French Quarter and had one of the upper floor apartments in a renovated antebellum hotel, located close to Jackson Square. Luke's luxury apartment overlooked the

Square, with a good view of the statue of Andrew Jackson rearing back on his steed, waving. Some say he was waving to his mistress, who had lived in the same hotel Luke now called home.

Unlocking the door to his apartment, Luke ushered Caroline in. "This is where I hang my hat. I like the location and the view. Seems like there's always something going on in Jackson Square, and living here makes me feel like I'm in the middle of it all."

"Quite a pad. Where did you find all of these antique pieces?" Caroline asked, as she gently ran her hand across the top of a Victorian end table.

"I'm fortunate enough to have a scout out there, always on the hunt," Luke said, as he patted the base of a large Tiffany stained glass lamp sitting on the end table. He crossed the room and opened the door to a bedroom. "This is the guest room. You can put your things down and make yourself comfortable. I'll make us a cup of hot chocolate."

"Now that's a switch. I haven't had hot chocolate, in ages. It's probably better for me than a double martini. Although, right now, I could use two triples. It's good to have someone keep me on the straight and narrow. Thank you, Luke, for being my guardian angel."

"Wouldn't want it another way. If you're up to it, I would like to try to contact Grant, tonight. He has made his presence known, and we need to see how all this is going to play out."

Caroline felt her stomach drop.

"I know it will be difficult for you, but no time is going to be the right time or better time. You have to face it, sometime, Caroline. It might as well be now."

"I know," Caroline said, in a hushed tone, twisting the tissue she was holding.

Luke headed to the galley kitchen, made elegant by a countertop of potted plants, a red-shaded miniature lamp, and a set of Mason jar canisters. He effortlessly prepared homemade hot chocolate, placed two black mugs on the kitchen counter, and poured steaming liquid into each.

"Whipped cream?" Caroline shook her head, and Luke picked up the mugs. Gesturing with his head, he beckoned her to follow him into the living room. She watched him gracefully balance the hot receptacles and set them on the glass top coffee table. After he handed her one, he took up his, and peered at her through the steam.

"It's now or never," he said.

"I…I'm scared. I don't know what to expect."

"If Grant wants to come through, he will. He will come through me, however. You needn't be afraid of anything."

"I trust you, but how does all this work? How are you able to communicate with the other side?"

"It's a process called channeling. I channel my energy to cross boundaries and connect with spiritual beings."

"How is that possible?"

"If you will allow me, I can help you with your emotional, physical, mental, and spiritual healing. We all have a team, that is, spiritual guides and angels. One of our goals will be to get you to recognize your team and the advantage of their assistance. Your team is a gift from God, and is here to promote your well-being. As a psychic medium, I will explore your past, present, and future and, thus, get a clearer picture of you. We will then use meditation to connect you with your angel and spiritual guides. I will communicate with your team and share the messages I receive from your guides."

Caroline's brow began to furrow, "Is it possible for me to connect directly with my, er, team?"

"Yes. We all have the ability to connect with our team. It's a level of psychic medium sense that has to be developed. Once you learn the process, you can connect and communicate with these spirits. Some positive signs to look for in detecting a spiritual presence are spirit dream visits—you have already experienced this. Also, you will experience unexplainable changes. For example, you put something down and know exactly where you left it. When you go to retrieve it, it isn't there. After searching for it and not finding it, you may later go back to the original spot and there it is, as if it had been there all along."

"Oh, my God! That happened with my car keys. I knew exactly where they were, but when I looked in the drawer they weren't there. That same afternoon, the afternoon I made the appointment with you, I did a thorough search of the house. Not finding them, I went back to the kitchen drawer where we always kept them. When I opened the drawer, just as you said, they were there, in plain sight. I attributed this to my being stressed and overlooking them the first time. I assume Grant is responsible for the shell game?"

"I would say yes. He is certainly trying to get your attention. From what you've disclosed to me, I'm sure you have experienced the third element of a spiritual presence. We call it 'unseen company.' Some of my clients reveal that they feel a quick shiver or get goose bumps for no apparent reason. Your sixth sense recognizes the presence of the spirit, and your body reacts."

"I wouldn't know sixth sense reaction from just plain fright, at this point. How do you contact the other side?"

"There are two types of mediums. Some go into a trance and, once the session is over and the medium awakens, he or she usually does not remember what transpired. I prefer to remain conscious. I listen and relay what I hear. My method of preparation is to become quiet and calm. This allows the spirit to come across." Luke set his mug down and took hers. "Are you ready?"

Holding her crossed fingers up for Luke to see, Caroline said, "Okay, let's do it."

Luke nodded. He sat back and laid his head against the sofa. Taking deep breaths, he closed his eyes and sighed. He appeared to be in a trance or in a different dimension. Then, without warning, he began to speak.

"Caroline, my love," he said, in a different, but familiar voice.

Caroline recognized the voice immediately. Grant's. She hurriedly tucked her legs up under her, transfixed and unsure of what to expect. Tears ran down her cheeks. Apprehension turned into excitement. Instead of separation, there was now a connection. She didn't know if that was something she wanted—especially now. However, there was no turning back.

"I want you to know there is a better place. However, because my life on earth was not fulfilled, I came back. You know what I want and you know how relentless I can be. Please, darling, don't fight this. You will be a famous concert pianist. Why wouldn't you want to, and at the same time fulfill my dream? Caroline, you really have no choice, you have no choice…you have no choice…"

Grant's voice diminished, and Luke gradually sat up. Caroline could see he was very tired. She watched him rub his neck and take a deep, cleansing breath. He said, "So, it's just as you already know. He wants to continue to play the piano through you. His expectations are that he, using you, will become world renowned."

Caroline was shaking. "What now? How can I convince him I don't want to do that? I want him to move on. To just leave me alone. He's not of this world. It scares me! His visits and control scare me! I don't like it and I don't want it! Please, Luke, please, please help me." She buried her face in her hands and wept. "Is this a bad dream? This can't really be happening, can it?"

Moving to sit beside her, Luke took her hands in his. "Don't worry, Caroline. It will be all right. We can and will discourage him, but it will take time. As you heard, he is relentless. Did he always get his way when he was alive?"

"Yes, always. I love…er, loved him, dearly, but he could be quite difficult, at times."

"I sensed that and I would like more details, but it's late, and I'm sorry to say, I'm done in. I want to sleep on the events of this evening, and assume you do, as well. We can explore our options, tomorrow."

"My sentiments, exactly." Then looking around, Caroline asked, "You wouldn't, by chance, have a spare pair of pajamas would you?"

"Never use them, but I do have a T-shirt that could double as a nightgown."

"That'll do. How 'bout one with the Saints logo on it?" She pointed to the one Luke was wearing. "I could use some saintly help."

In his best John Wayne imitation, Luke said, "Well, pilgrim, since you got separated from the wagon train, 'spect I could 'commodate ya." He hitched up his jeans with his forearms, John Wayne style, and swaggered off toward his bedroom.

Caroline shook her head and chuckled. Luke came back with an armload of Saints T-shirts. "And, what's that old saying, 'What do you get the man who has everything?' Beats silly neckties. Take your pick." He held up an array of shirts for her to inspect.

After making her selection, Caroline asked, "Do you mind if I leave the door to my room open. I am too frightened to relax."

"You have nothing to fear from the spirits, but yes, if it is comforting, leave your door open, and I will, too," Luke reassured her. "I keep extra toothbrushes in the vanity drawers in the spare bathroom. Help yourself. There's a terry robe hanging on the back of the bathroom door, too. You're welcome to use it and anything else you may need."

Caroline nodded and stood up on shaky legs. She tripped over the coffee table, and Luke jumped to help her. She waved him off. "I'm okay, just getting my bearings. Thank you, Luke, for everything. See you in the morning."

"Yes, in the morning."

CHAPTER
5

Luke was scrambling eggs into an omelet, when Caroline finally emerged from the guest room. She was wearing the proffered terry robe and rubbing sleep from her eyes. "Something smells good," she said, as she slipped onto a stool at the counter in the kitchen.

"You're in for a treat. I'm preparing my specialty. It's a Cajun omelet that was taught to me by an old family friend. When I say old, I mean old. Think she may have been a hundred, back then. Maybe the ingredients in the omelet are what keep her going."

"She's still alive?"

"Yep, and going strong. Are you willing to chance my creation?"

"Damn straight. Hunger is the driving force here. I could eat a horse."

"Ah, we won't go that far. Pig is the order of the day, Sea Biscuit is quite safe. What we have here is bacon and sausage combined with potatoes, peppers, onion, and a plethora of secret ingredients designed to tantalize the taste buds."

"You're torturing me. Hurry it up," Caroline coaxed, as she poured a cup of coffee.

WHEN THEY finished eating, Caroline helped Luke clean the breakfast dishes. "You're prediction proved to be correct. That was the best omelet I've ever eaten."

"Nectar of the gods; you'll learn to trust me," Luke said, as he wiped off the counter with the damp dishcloth. "I do not schedule appointments on Fridays unless it's an emergency. So, with that in mind, we have the whole day to prepare you for upcoming events."

"You make it sound like a social function."

"I apologize if you thought I was making light of the situation. It's important I have some history to shore up my interaction with Grant. Sit down and tell me more about yourself." Luke slid onto one of the stools at the kitchen counter, propped his chin on his palms, and his eyes probed her expression.

"I'm afraid you'll be bored to death," Caroline said, sitting down across from him. She paused and took a sip of coffee before she continued, "Well, here goes. As you already know, The Senator, my father, was scarce during my childhood– and still is, for that matter. I think he was present more the three months I was in the hospital than he had been my entire life. Paul tells me Dad was constantly by my bedside. That was a comfort to me because, quite frankly, I didn't have anyone, except Paul, and he isn't exactly a blood relative.

"I don't know much about my mother. Mostly my recollection of her is what Dad has told me. She was a Vassar graduate, and he met her at a West Point dance. He, of course, went to West Point and was a cadet when they met. Dad was struck dumb by Mother's beauty and, according to him, the two embarked on a whirlwind courtship that resulted in Dad proposing to Mother in the chapel at West Point. They were married within six months of their meeting. Nettie—that's my nanny—filled in some blanks for me. She told me The Senator idolized my mother. Her name was Virginia," Caroline said, smiling, "and Dad was adamant about calling her by her Christian name. No nicknames, thank you very much! He wouldn't let anyone call her Virgie or Ginny."

Luke nodded his head, "Go on."

"Nettie had been employed by Dad's family for years, and when my parents married, she was part of the endowment. But, don't get the wrong idea. Slavery died with Lincoln. Nettie was offered the opportunity to be employed by the newlyweds, and she agreed to do so. She was paid well for her services. She had been nursemaid to The Senator and then to me, after I was born." Caroline looked down, a sad expression replaced the glow. Caroline brushed away tears with her fingers. "Nettie died about two years ago. It was like losing my mother, all over again." She sniffed.

Luke handed her a tissue and coaxed. "Go on, Caroline."

Caroline dabbed at her eyes. "Nettie was a treasure chest of history, having been employed by the Schumann family for so many years. She related stories depicting Mother as quite the socialite who entertained on a grand scale. She embellished on the parties Dad and Mother threw that 'they're still talking about.'

"Mother was only twenty-nine when she contacted yellow fever. The symptoms were much like the flu, and so it was diagnosed as such. You see, there hadn't been a case of yellow fever reported in years. By the time it was determined she had yellow fever, it was too late."

Luke interrupted, "What a tragedy to die so young, and it could have been prevented. Did you say you were four when she died?"

"Yes, that's right. That was twenty-five years ago. Nettie told me how hard Dad took Mother's death. He locked himself in his den and didn't come out for days. When he did reappear, he reeked of unwashed body, stale alcohol, and cigar smoke. Nettie said Mother's death changed him— and not for the better. From then on, he was sullen and depressed most of the time. She often told me I was the picture of my mother. She also suspected I was a strong reminder of his loss. So, The Senator sent me to a boarding school."

"That's harsh. Do you remember how that affected you?"

"I was six at the time, but even at such a young age, I knew I was being uprooted from the life I knew, people who loved me, and those I loved. Leaving familiar surroundings had quite an impact on me. I became defiant and rebellious. Nettie told me later the school telephoned The Senator, almost weekly, complaining about my behavior. The Senator always won and he had the means to get his way in almost everything, except…except Mother's death. I think that's why her death devastated him so much. It was something he couldn't pay to fix."

"Interesting. How is your relationship with your father, now? I notice you refer to him interchange-ably as 'The Senator' and 'Dad,' but you seem to have a difficult time calling him the latter."

"Now?" She took a deep breath. "Now that I'm older and much wiser, I understand more than I ever thought I could. I've lived, loved, and lost. I forgave my father long before Grant died. I eventually realized Dad's life must have been hell, for years. I learned a lot going to boarding school, and not all of it was academic. The school I attended was for the rich and privileged. You can imagine, if you have no consequences for your actions, what's to keep you from doing exactly what you like? And, we did. I'm ashamed of some of the pranks we pulled on the instructors, but at the time, teenage hormones ruled. We thought we were pretty clever. Me and my colleagues snuck out at night and had rendezvous with the students from the rich and privileged boy's academy, across the Mississippi."

"Think I get the picture. Did your father ever come to visit you at school?"

"Very seldom. I went home for the holidays and summer break. He eventually warmed up to me and now, well now, at least we're friends. And, you're right. I do have difficulty calling my father 'Dad.' Calling him The Senator distances me from him and the emotions that go with it. Calling him The Senator makes our relationship more impersonal, and our separation more tolerable."

Luke leaned forward and rested his crossed arms on the counter. "How did you meet Grant?"

Caroline rubbed her brow, before she said, "I met Grant at a concert in New Orleans where I attended Tulane. The Senator came to the Big Easy, occasionally. I suspected he had a female friend he came to see, and used me as an excuse to protect his reputation. He took me to a symphony where Grant was the featured pianist. Because of The Senator's privileged status, we were escorted backstage to meet the musicians. That's when I met Grant. He swept me off my feet and was relentless in his pursuit. We were married in Charleston, a year later, after I received my law degree. Our wedding was spectacular, The Senator put on quite the show. Our relationship at that time was still tenuous. I had to grow and experience life on my own before I was able to understand Dad and the ghosts he fought."

"And, did you?"

"Yes. We didn't see each other much during the three years I was married to Grant, but I forgave him."

"Did you talk to him about it?"

"Yes, well, we skirted around the issue during one of his visits, shortly before the accident. It was difficult for either one of us to say 'I forgive you,' however, we both knew we were forgiven."

"How so?"

"His attitude changed. He wasn't so standoffish, and I softened towards him. He had given me a pretty large dowry and his generosity did not go unappreciated. I made sure he knew how grateful we were. We bought our mansion, thanks to Dad, and were able to live on what Grant made with the symphony. I never had the chance to use my degree."

Caroline got up and put her coffee cup in the dishwasher.

Luke asked, "Is that something you regret? Not having the opportunity to use your law degree, that is."

"At the time, no. I was happy being the wife of a famous pianist. We were very much in love and were married less than two years, before the accident. This spirit that is haunting me isn't the

Grant I thought I knew. I never detected he was on a mission to 'set the world on fire.'

"Now, with twenty-twenty hindsight, I wish I had pursued a legal career. Not so much for income. I'm well taken care of. However, I regret not having done something useful with *my* life, and I don't mean *his* desire to use me to fulfill *his* dreams. I carried a four-point all seven years I attended universities. I love the law and wanted to be a prosecutor. Don't go making something out of that. It isn't a vendetta. I wanted to be on the side of justice in the criminal arena. I found civil law to be pretty boring, and being a defense attorney never appealed to me. I couldn't get used to defending those I knew to be guilty."

"I'm not here to judge you, Caroline." Luke rose and poured himself another cup of coffee. "I'm not a psychiatrist, I'm a psychic. I just want a true and complete picture of your past and present. It's important to your future. So, Shahrazad, continue."

"Shahrazad? Don't know if I like that. She could have come to a very bad end."

"Indeed—but she didn't. Her perseverance saved her life," Luke smiled, and lifted his cup in a salute, before taking a drink.

"You made your point. I guess I am defensive to some degree. I'm running scared and, well, maybe I'm a trifle bitter. It seems whenever something good happens in my life, it's short-lived."

"We all have to deal with what life throws at us. You're not unique, in that respect."

"I suppose not. You say you want to understand my past, and I'm trying to tell you in my own words how I feel or felt at the time. Losing Grant was devastating, but facing death, myself, was extremely traumatic, both physically and emotionally. I wished often during the three months of recovery that I, too, would die. Having Dad by my bedside gave me the courage to go on. At least he was there when I needed him most. I don't remember, if I ever knew, how many reconstructive surgeries I underwent. I was in constant pain and grieving over Grant, at the same time. I wasn't even allowed to attend Grant's funeral! So," she leaned back against her seat, "basically, I've had no closure."

"Do you think—?"

"Think what? That I conjured all of this up? You sat right there and conveyed Grant's message. So, what do you think? Am I a fraud? Is this some elaborate scheme, and if so, to what end?" After a pause, she added, "Maybe I should go."

"Caroline, settle down. That's not what I was driving at. My question was do you think you'll be able to stand up to him and not capitulate to his demands? He is a spirit, after all, and should not be able to control your actions. You have a free will."

Caroline felt momentarily guilty. "Sorry if I misunderstood you, Luke." She tugged on her lower lip. "So, if what you're saying is true, where's all that free will, when he forces me to play the piano? I don't want to be his pawn. I'm just helpless to resist."

"As I told you, I'll have to do some research." Luke reached a hand over and covered hers. "Look, it's almost noon. I think we've done enough, for now. How do you feel about going home?"

"I have to face it, sometime, so I may as well just do it. Luke, I felt pretty hopeless when I came to see you. You've given me hope. I promise I'll work on an attitude adjustment and, with your help, find the solution to this dilemma." Caroline rose from the bar stool. "I'll get dressed, so we can leave."

Conversation on the way to Caroline's centered on some childhood experiences of Luke's and his close encounters with the spirit world. Caroline felt a strong connection with him and she thought he felt it back. There was a comfortable rapport that she hadn't experienced since Grant was alive. *Hmm, perhaps there might be something more than professionalism in the future with this handsome and kind man.*

MOVEMENT TWO
RHAPSODY

CHAPTER

6

After Luke dropped Caroline at her front door, she entered her home with a sense of trepidation. *What if Grant is waiting in the foyer for me—a specter with crossed arms and tapping toe?* Caroline bravely brushed the image from her mind, straightened her shoulders, and forged towards the kitchen with only a slight desire to run for her life. She wondered if her imagination was working overtime as a coping mechanism to soften the blow of having lost a spouse.

Caroline, although apprehensive, entered the kitchen. She noticed the light on her answering machine blinking wildly, but chose to ignore it, at least for the time being. Leaving the kitchen, she completed her tour through the house to satisfy herself all was in order. She started her laundry and went to the pantry to assess what she needed from the grocery. While preparing a list she glanced at the telephone. The blinking light still beckoned to her, so she punched the play button to pick up her calls. The first one was from Paul Bruno.

"Caroline, I came by this morning. I called a couple of times last evening when I got home, but you didn't answer. I was concerned so I dropped by your place on my way to the office. When I didn't find you at home my anxiety piqued. I don't want to monitor your life or be labeled a babysitter, but I truly am anxious about your well-being. Call me as soon as you receive this message."

Holy crap. I hope he didn't call The Senator. Caroline grabbed up the phone and hurriedly dialed Paul's number.

"This is Paul Bruno. I'm either out of the office or with a patient. Please leave a message, including your name and the nature of your call. I will return your call as soon as possible. Thank you."

Caroline sat drumming her fingernails on the countertop, as she waited for the answering machine to kick in. *Finally!* "Paul, this is Caroline. I'm fine. I, er, I was out late last night and left early this morning to get some shopping done—beat the crowd and all that, you know. I apologize for worrying you. It was needless, and I'm doing well. Please don't put me in the position of having to check in-and-out with you every time I leave the house. But, thank you for your concern."

Caroline ended the call. She listened to the next three messages which were from friends inquiring about her well-being. The fifth message startled her. It was from Edwardo, the conductor of the orchestra.

"Caroline, the orchestra is preparing a special arrangement for this coming Saturday's performance. You were not aware, but some months before the accident, Grant asked me if we would include a number for your upcoming thirtieth birthday. He wanted to surprise you and he knew you loved Carroll Multz' music. He even jokingly said when we discussed it, 'Wish she loved my music as much as she does his.' He selected what he determined to be your favorite musical composition, *Turn Back To Me,* from Multz' most current CD.

"We, that is, the orchestra want to honor Grant's wish and dedicate the next performance to his memory. We've done a workup conforming to Grant's specifications. He had been working on this project several weeks before the accident and had it perfected. We want to incorporate this number in Saturday's performance and would very much like for you to attend as the guest, since the number is in your honor."

Caroline heard the beep indicating the battery was running low. She surmised Edwardo must have also heard it, as he rushed through the rest of his message.

"Please let me know as soon as possible if you can make it. We're counting on you being available to attend and help us celebrate Grant's life and remarkable talent. Plus, we want to see you.

We miss you and your occasional visits to our rehearsals."

When the message ended, Caroline dropped the receiver into its cradle. Numb, she walked up the stairs to her bedroom and curled up on her bed.

"Oh, Grant, I wish I could trade places with you. You had so much to live for. Edwardo told me what you planned for my birthday. I'm touched and, boy, would I have been surprised, especially after you told me time-and-again you'd never play a Multz composition.

"After what happened at *The Cotton Club*, how can I attend? I know what you intend to do. I'm pleading with you. If you ever loved me, please don't continue to torment me. Please, please let me be."

Caroline suddenly jumped up and ran down stairs. *I can't handle this alone. I need to talk to Luke.* She went to the kitchen drawer to retrieve the car keys only to find them missing. Again! She shuffled the contents of the drawer around. *I'm sure I put them here. Oh, no!* She remembered Luke's exact words the day before. "Another indication of a spirit's presence is unexplainable changes. For example, you put something down and know exactly where that object is, but when you go to retrieve it, it isn't there." She looked down at the drawer in dread.

The ringing of the phone caused her to flinch. She grabbed the receiver, "Hello."

"Caroline, I've been worried sick about you," Paul said. "When I wasn't able to reach you last night, I almost called the hospitals—"

"You didn't!"

"Well, I was tempted."

"Really, Paul, I'm doing just fine. Your suggestion that familiar surroundings would be beneficial was brilliant. I'm feeling more and more like my old self. I apologize for worrying you. Please don't make me feel like a teenager with a curfew, though. I really can take care of myself."

"Then it is I who should be apologizing. It wasn't my intention to be a busybody. It's just that I promised your father I would watch over you, and when you went missing, I panicked. I'll try to reign in my fatherly nature in the future and be more circumspect. Now that we have that out of the way, are you free for lunch?"

"Well, I…"

"It's settled. I'll come by a little before noon. We'll try the country club, again, but this time I'll pick you up." He barked a laugh. "No chance for you to stand me up, then!"

Caroline rolled her eyes. "Heh, I'll be ready."

SHE WAS leaning against the entryway doorjamb when Paul pulled into the driveway. After checking to make sure the front door was locked behind her, she walked to his Lexus. Ever the gentleman, Paul stood by the open passenger door. She scooted onto the tan leather seat and pulled the safety belt over her shoulder.

"You look tired. Have you been sleeping?" Paul said, after he'd slid behind the steering wheel.

"Why yes. I sleep just fine. In fact, I could give Snow White competition in the sleep department." Setting her Gucci purse at her feet, she continued, "I'm still recovering and I suppose that takes its toll on me."

"Your reconstruction has healed nicely, hardly noticeable. When is your follow up appointment?"

Caroline touched the spot on her neck. The scar had been removed and now all that remained was redness which was gradually vanishing. She answered Paul, "Um, sometime next month. My surgeon certainly knew his stuff. I don't have any visible scars."

"Yes, The Senator had heard of Dr. Winebury and was adamant he be consulted. Upon reviewing your injuries, Winebury insisted he perform the surgeries, himself."

"Yes, I know." *And, for an exorbitant fee.* "I'm grateful to Dad for all of that."

"Well, you should be. It would be nice if you kept in closer touch with him. He's getting up in years, you know."

Caroline was silent.

Paul, changing the subject, awkwardly asked, "Are you hungry?" He shot her a sidelong glance.

She was beginning to feel uncomfortable at being interrogated, and answered, "Starved. I haven't been to the country club, in months."

"The staff is pretty much the same. However, they have a new chef, Andre."

"That's original."

"Quite."

"Do all chefs go by the same moniker?"

"Seemingly so, but you'll find this one is unique and quite talented. I think you'll like his creations."

"I'm sure I will."

When they were seated, and after the waitress took their orders, Paul said, "Edwardo called yesterday."

Caroline suddenly felt lightheaded. "Yes, he called me, as well." She cleared her throat.

"I think it's wonderful they want to honor Grant with the special number he arranged as a surprise for your birthday. What do you think?"

"Yes, that is wonderful."

"You don't seem to be very enthusiastic. You are going to go, aren't you?"

"Um, if I can."

"IF YOU CAN! Perhaps I don't understand what you mean, 'if you can.'"

"No, that's not what I meant." *Good God, how am I going to get out this?*

"Well, I certainly hope not. Can you imagine the disappointment of not having you attend as the guest of honor at a symphony dedicated to your husband's memory, and the WPSO playing your favorite musical composition at his request?"

Caroline murmured something unintelligible and picked at her food. The rest of the meal was consumed in awkward silence.

AFTER LUNCH, Paul took Caroline home. As soon as he left, Caroline went to the kitchen drawer and, no surprise, there were her car keys. She sat down at the counter and buried her head in her hands, wanting to wail. As much as she had hoped it was all in her mind, this really was happening! She needed to see Luke! Making that decision comforted her, somewhat. She grabbed the keys from the drawer and ran to the garage. *I should call him first, but even if he's busy, I'll wait.*

Caroline made the trip from her home to the French Quarter in record time. She entered Luke's office and, seeing his private office door was closed, she took a seat. Fifteen minutes into her wait the door opened, and Luke appeared, escorting an older woman toward the exit. Smiling at Caroline, he turned toward his client and said, "Well, Mrs. Sinclair, since we determined Oliver is happy, and that he doesn't want you to worry about him, anymore, I hope your mind's at ease. He obviously wants you to get on with your life."

"Oh, it was comforting to hear he's happy, and our session did ease my fears. I'm so relieved, Mr. Luke, I can't thank you enough. You know, Oliver wasn't the best husband in the world, but he was the only husband I ever had, and I miss him. I worried about his soul. Now I can rest knowing he is happy in the afterlife."

"Good!" Luke opened the outer door and held it for the woman. "Call me if you need to talk."

"I will and thank you, again. Good day, now."

Closing the door, Luke turned toward Caroline and said, "I'm happy to see you, but I sense something happened to bring you here this afternoon."

"Yes, there's a crisis."

Luke gestured toward the door, "That was my last appointment for the day, Come in. What kind of crisis are we talking about?"

Caroline followed Luke to his private office and slumped in the now familiar chair she'd occupied before. Luke pulled a chair next to her. Taking her hand, he said, "Come on, what is it?"

Caroline related the substance of Edwardo's phone call and then lunch with Paul. She concluded by adding, "I just can't do it. You know what'll happen."

"Yes, your fears are well-grounded. But, on the other hand, how can you not attend?"

"Exactly. Guess I could get the flu or break a leg…"

"Whoa! Don't do anything that drastic."

Then after a few moments of thoughtful reflection, Luke said, "I have a plan. I'll go as your escort and hang on to you like there's no tomorrow. Even if Grant tries to manipulate you, I'll keep you under physical restraint."

"Do you think that'll work?"

"I'm pretty strong and, yes, I think that will work."

"Paul wants to go with me, as well. I don't want him to know about Grant's visits. How will we get around that?"

"Hmm, let me think." Luke rubbed the back of his neck for a moment. "Ah! Perhaps I won't have to hang onto you physically, the entire time. I'll just keep an eye on you, and if it looks like a reenactment of *The Cotton Club*, I'll take your arm to keep you from rising from your seat. Will you have a box or front row seating?"

"Don't know for sure but, in the past, special guests were given a box overlooking the stage. From Edwardo's message, it sounds like a grand production, so I think a box would be more likely. I don't mind telling you, I'm frightened at the thought of what may happen."

"Understandably so. Try not to dwell on it. It'll be okay—I promise."

"Do you know that from experience, or is that supposition on your part?"

"A little of both. Let's try to contact Grant and get a feel for what he plans."

Caroline was not eager to contact Grant so she said, "You don't really believe he would reveal anything, do you? I tried to speak to him earlier, begging him to leave me alone, but didn't get a response."

"That's disquieting. He may not want to communicate with you until after the symphony.

We'll give it a try, anyway." After a slight pause, Luke said, "Are you ready?"

"Yes…and no." She finally acquiesced. " Why not?"

Luke nodded to her and leaned his head back and became very still. His breathing slowed and his eyes closed. He remained in that position for several minutes, while Caroline watched. Finally, Luke opened his eyes. "I'm not getting anything. My guess is he doesn't want to reveal himself for fear we will spoil his plan."

"Is that good or bad?"

"Not good, but we also have a plan. When is the symphony?"

"Saturday at Tulane's Concert Center, starting at seven-thirty."

"I'll pick you up at five-thirty. We'll have a light dinner and arrive there early enough to get situated. That will give us time to size-up the situation. Do you want to invite Paul to dinner, or better, just have him meet us there?"

"As nervous as I will probably be, I prefer just meeting him there. And, really, thank you for the invitation, but I don't think I would be able to eat anything, considering the circumstances. Can you pick me up at six-thirty? That will give us time to establish some type of counter attack."

"Counter attack! That's a good description and very appropriate. Yes, I can do that. Since you refused my invitation for dinner on Saturday, how 'bout we grab a bite, now? I know it's early, but I'm famished."

"I'd like that. I couldn't eat, earlier. Paul and I had a misunderstanding, and I lost my appetite. Suddenly, I'm also hungry and I'm not anxious to go home, just yet."

"I haven't made the bed in the spare room. It's still yours, if you want it."

"Good Lord. Between you and Paul, I'm beginning to feel like a baby."

Throwing his hands in the air, Luke shouted, "HOY! I give up."

"Hoy? Are you that exasperated?"

"Yes! Come on; let's go. What sounds good? Seafood, Italian, Chinese, or Creole?"

"All of the above. You decide since you're the exasperated one."

Luke laughed, as he opened the door and ushered Caroline out into the corridor. He was still shaking his head, when they pulled into traffic.

CHAPTER

7

Caroline called Edwardo as soon as she returned home.

"Edwardo, I'm pleased to have caught you and apologize for the lateness of returning your call."

"Nonsense! We assumed you would accept our invitation and come, so we have been planning for you. You do intend to attend, don't you?"

"Why, yes. And, thank you and the symphony for honoring Grant in this manner. I know he will, er, would have been pleased."

"Oh, my, yes. He surely would have been pleased. We have created a special set for the occasion. However, I'm not going to tell you about it and spoil the surprise."

Damn, wouldn't you just know it—a special set. Wonder what that's all about. Anyway, I'm going to be safely tucked between Paul and Luke, so it doesn't matter, anyway. "How nice that you've gone to so much trouble."

"Not at all! Grant was a superb pianist and a cherished member of this orchestra. We want this to be a memorable occasion."

"Looking forward to it," Caroline cringed, embarrassed by the pretext. "I have to go now and make another call," she said. "See you Saturday evening."

"I'll have front row tickets waiting at the ticket window for you and any guests. How many tickets will you need?"

"Ah, three, three of us will be attending. Did you say front row seating?"

"Yes. Our special set obscures the stage from the box seats, so they're closed off for this performance. I speak for the entire orchestra when I say we're looking forward to seeing you once again. You light up the whole auditorium with your presence."

"You're too kind, thank you for the compliment. Until Saturday."

"Yes, until Saturday."

After terminating the call, Caroline telephoned Paul. He didn't answer, so she left a message.

"Paul, this is Caroline. I just talked to Edwardo, and he will be leaving tickets at the box office for us. I will meet you at the auditorium around seven, Saturday evening, by the ticket window. I'm coming with a, ah, er, a friend, so there will be three tickets. Please call me if your plans have changed. Otherwise, I'll see you Saturday."

Too bad we can't have box seating. A box would be better but it isn't going to make any difference anyway. We have a plan. Caroline was exhausted, as she prepared for bed. After taking a shower, she went downstairs and poured herself a tall glass of mixed juice. Earlier, she had decided to keep the car keys in her shoulder bag hoping to keep Grant from moving them. On a whim, on her way back to her bedroom, she stopped by the drawer where she usually deposited the car keys. She wasn't sure she believed a spirit could move things so, subconsciously, she was testing Luke's theory even knowing the keys were safe in her bag. She slid the drawer open and stared wide-eyed at the keys, which were right there, in plain sight.

Caroline slammed the drawer shut and shouted, "Grant, it's done! You cannot make me do your bidding. No matter what you do, I will not do it! Besides, how does my playing make you famous? Don't you see, it would be me, not you! You're driving me mad with your games! If you ever loved me, please, please leave me alone. I feel like I'm imprisoned. You've taken my life away! I may as well be dead, if this is how I have to live! Damn it, Grant, I won't have it!"

Caroline wilted after her tirade. She went into the drawing room and reclined on the sofa. She pulled the wool throw around her shoulders and was instantly asleep. When she awoke the next morning, she remembered the dream she'd had. Grant had spoken to her while she slept.

I did love you with all my heart. I still do. Don't fight me, my darling. Get used to the idea. Caroline. You will *do what I ask. You have no choice..."*

She shivered at the voice that still echoed in her mind. *My God, what am I to do?*

IT WAS Friday, and the symphony was just one day away. Caroline could barely find the energy to brush her teeth, let alone face the long day ahead of her. She called Luke to tell him about the dream and seek consolation.

"Caroline, what Grant doesn't get is that you *do* have a choice. We all have free will and free agency. We are able to make choices! You choose not to play, and we have a plan to implement that choice, even if Grant thinks otherwise."

"It sounds to me like he *knows* otherwise. By the way, we have front row seating. It appears the orchestra has an elaborate set for Saturday's performance, which would obstruct patrons in the boxes from seeing the stage."

"It doesn't matter. Our plan will work, no matter where we're seated. We'll sandwich you in between Paul and me, so you would have to crawl over one of us to get out. Even though Paul doesn't know about Grant's visits, if you start to get up, that would give me time to react and restrain you. Try not to fret and be upset."

"You make it sound so simple. I have to trust you—I have nowhere else to turn. Will you still be picking me up at six-thirty?"

"Yes, of course."

SATURDAY, THE first day of May, dawned bright and promising. Caroline had not dreamt, nor had Grant visited her since the night before. Her spirits were buoyed when she recounted her conversation with Luke. *Perhaps by spoiling Grant's scheme tonight, he will get the message and leave me alone.* She went to the walk-in closet and selected a gown of black chiffon with a long flowing skirt. She hung it on the door hook, and then picked out the jewelry she'd wear, a simple garnet pendant on a long silver chain, and matching earrings. After pulling a pair of black sandals out and placing them below the dress, she stood back and admired her selection.

Satisfied, Caroline went to the kitchen, made a pot of coffee and toasted an English muffin. Just as she was sitting down to eat her breakfast, the doorbell rang. Hastening to answer, she peered out the long narrow window adjacent to the front entrance and saw a truck from one of the local florists parked in her driveway. She opened the door.

"Good morning," she said, greeting the delivery boy.

"Good morning, ma'am. I have a delivery for…" the delivery boy looked at his clip board, then continued, "for a Caroline Alexander."

"That would be me," Caroline replied, as she took the small corsage box and signed the form the boy offered her. She then retrieved a $5.00 bill from the jar on the table in the foyer and gave it to the delivery boy.

"Wow! Thank you, ma'am!"

"You're welcome," Caroline said, before she closed the door. She looked through the cellophane window of the small box and saw a lovely corsage of three white gardenias bound with a turquoise satin ribbon. She turned the box over, looking for a card, but found none. *Must be Paul. He knows I love gardenias… and turquoise. How thoughtful. I'll call the florist to make sure it was Paul. Wouldn't want to embarrass him if they weren't from him. Why, they could even be from Luke!*

Caroline dialed the number imprinted on the box under the name *Regal Flowers*.

"*Regal Flowers*, good morning. This is Rita. How may I help you?"

"Good morning, Rita. My name is Caroline Alexander and I just received a lovely corsage of white gardenias. There was no card attached to the package. Can you tell me who ordered them, so I can thank the sender?"

"I'm sorry, Ms. Alexander. It's against company policy to give out that information."

"Oh, really? Well then, could the card have come off during delivery?"

"That's unlikely. We securely attach our cards with a ribbon just because of the eventuality."

"So, there's no way I can find out who sent them?"

"Not unless the sender comes forward. We do have anonymous deliveries from time-to-time. It's not that unusual. I'm sorry I can't be of help to you."

After a slight pause, Caroline murmured, "Thank you, Rita, for your time."

"No thanks necessary. Have a good day."

Caroline hung up the phone. *What the hell?*

SATURDAY EVENING, Luke arrived at Caroline's, as scheduled. When she opened the door, Luke took a quick breath and said, "Well, just look at you. You look stunning."

"I don't feel stunning." Caroline turned and walked back into the foyer. She picked up the box and said, "I was delivered a corsage this morning without a card. You wouldn't have been the one who sent it, would you?"

"Why, no. Probably your friend, Paul. But, wish I had thought of it."

"I don't think it was Paul. He would have wanted the credit. I called the florist, but it's against their policy to reveal a sender if the sender requests to remain anonymous. Paul would not have made that request. Would Grant have the ability to do something like that?"

"I've heard of people receiving, um, say something like a rose that appears from nowhere. But, having a corsage delivered… You're not wearing it. May I see it?"

"Of course, come in." As Luke entered, Caroline handed him the box containing the corsage. Luke examined it, thoroughly. Suddenly, his back stiffened, and he began to speak. Chills coursed through Caroline's nerve endings, as she instantly recognized the voice. Grant!

"Caroline, why aren't you wearing the gardenias I sent? They're your favorite. Surely you intend to wear the corsage to the symphony. It's preordained."

Caroline tried to speak, but her voice was stuck in her throat, choking her. Just then, Luke leaned forward and awkwardly placed his hands on the table knocking a vase to the floor in the process. He shook his head, as if trying to loosen Grant's grip on his mind. Finally, his eyes cleared, and he peered at Caroline.

"Are you okay?"

"I—I." Caroline was relieved to hear herself speak. "What the hell was that?" She glanced at the flower box and grabbed it and ran to the kitchen. She stood at the kitchen sink and tore the flowers into little bits and crammed them down the garbage disposal. "This is what I think of your corsage, Grant!" She flipped the disposal on and whipped around to face Luke, who was standing at the doorway with an astonished look on his face.

He walked over and flipped the switch off. "I think they are as decimated as they can get."

Trying to catch her breath, she said, "I'm sending Grant a return message!" Before she knew it, she was in Luke's arms and sobbing into his shoulder. It felt so good to let it all out.

Luke stroked the back of her neck until the storm passed. Luke then lifted her chin gently and cradled her damp face in his hands. "It's getting late. We have to leave soon, to make it on time."

"I'm not going! I can't go through with the charade. It's a setup! The WPHO is an unwitting pawn in Grant's hands. He may be able to maneuver them, but not me. I won't let him do this to me! You said it! He has no power over me, unless I give it to him."

Luke handed her a tissue and then another one. "It's got to be done, Caroline. You'll be secure enough, sandwiched between Paul and me. The orchestra is counting on you being there. But, if you insist, we won't go. I don't want you to be troubled, anymore."

Caroline slumped against him. "Thank you for your concern." She sniffled and continued, "I suppose you're right. You promise you won't let anything happen?"

"Yes, I promise. Scouts honor," Luke said, and held up two fingers on his right hand sealing the oath, Boy Scout style. "Now, go fix your face and grab a wrap." He tapped the face of his watch with his forefinger, his stern face managing to look apologetic.

PAUL WAS waiting at the ticket window when Caroline and Luke arrived.

"There you are! I was beginning to wonder. Caroline, you look lovely."

"Thank you, Paul. Did you get the tickets?"

"Yes, right here," Paul replied holding up the tickets. "We have front row seats—front row center, to be exact."

Caroline noticed Paul's furtive glance in Luke's direction, and said, "Paul, I'd like you to meet Quinton Lucas, a friend of mine." She turned to Luke and introduced him to Paul.

Luke extended his hand and said, "I'm happy to finally meet you. Caroline speaks of you often."

Paul replied, "All good, I hope. It's a pleasure to meet you, as well." He looked at Caroline then Luke, and Caroline could see Paul was trying to figure out their relationship.

"Yes, it's all good. Caroline raves when she speaks of you. And, she is so appreciative of your helping her after the tragic accident."

"Those were dark days. The Senator, Caroline's father, and I go way back. We went to West Point, together. Where did you say you know Caroline from?"

"Caroline told me the history of you and her father," Luke said, sidestepping Paul's question. He nodded in Caroline's direction.

"Yes. We go back a long way. I knew Caroline's parents before she was born," Paul replied, squinting. "Now, where did you say you met Caroline?" he persisted.

At that moment Caroline intruded, "Hey, you two. Don't talk about me as if I weren't here. We need to get seated. It sounds like the orchestra is warming up."

"Right you are." Paul took Caroline's arm and nodded to Luke, as he escorted her to their seats. Luke followed close behind.

Once they were seated, Caroline commented, "These are great seats." She, however, was seated on the outside next to Paul. "Do you mind, Paul, if we change places? I'd like to sit between the two of you. After all, it isn't often I'm accompanied by two handsome gents."

"Certainly." Paul frowned. A brief moment of distaste flitted across his features but disappeared quickly. "Here, let me help you."

Caroline, settling into her new seat, heard Luke groan next to her.

"What is it?" Caroline asked in a worried voice.

Luke handed his open program to Caroline. Her eyes narrowed as she read,

Westchester Philharmonic Symphony Orchestra dedicates tonight's performance to the memory of Grant Alexander, a long-time lead pianist of the WPSO.

Grant recently lost his life in a tragic automobile accident, but his music lives on. Months before his death, he requested we perform a special arrangement of Turn Back to Me that was to be dedicated to his wife, Caroline, for her 30th birthday. Our arrangement featured Grant at the piano.

Even though Grant is not with us physically, we want to fulfill his wish and dedicate our arrangement of Turn Back to Me *to his lovely wife, Caroline. Our soloist this evening, in Grant's absence, will be Victor Saville.*

Before Caroline had time to reply, the curtain opened, exposing the seated orchestra. All the members, even the women, were wearing white tuxedos. A mural depicting the New Orleans night skyline was the backdrop. As the curtain slid further toward the proscenium, two white grand pianos positioned center stage became visible. Caroline gasped and grabbed Luke's arm.

Luke patted her hand and whispered, "We have a plan, remember?"

Edwardo walked out onto the stage looking very handsome and professional in his contrasting black tuxedo. He faced the audience and bowed.

"Good evening ladies and gentlemen. Welcome to our symphonic tribute to the late Grant Alexander. If you have had time to look at the program, you will notice one of the arrangements we've prepared for this evening will be dedicated to Caroline, Grant's widow. Caroline is with us tonight as our guest of honor. Please welcome her."

The audience applauded.

"Stand up, Caroline," Edwardo encouraged. "Better yet, come on up here."

"No! I mean, please…" Caroline pleaded, but to no avail. The audience clapped louder.

Caroline clung to Luke desperately, as Edwardo descended the stage steps, holding out his hand. He walked up to her and beckoned her to join him. He took her by the hand and pulled her past Paul to the aisle. She felt him tugging at her hand and tried to hold back. When they reached the stage the audience was standing and the noise was deafening. Her eyes found Luke's, and he shrugged his shoulders, helplessly.

Standing center stage with Caroline beside him, Edwardo raised his hands to quiet the audience. When calm was restored, he said, "Caroline, the reason we have two pianos will become apparent to you momentarily." Edwardo led Caroline over to one of the grand pianos.

"This is the one Grant used during our performances here in New Orleans. Would you like to sit there, while we perform the arrangement Grant selected and wished to be dedicated to you?"

"NO! I mean, not really."

"Don't be shy. Grant would have wanted you to do so."

Don't I know it! "Please, Edwardo, I'm much too emotional to be on display," Caroline whispered, as she turned and started to walk away. "I'll just go back to my seat."

Edwardo grabbed her by the hand. *Can't the man take a hint, for goodness sakes? Apparently not.* He whispered back, "We expect you to be emotional. Why wouldn't you be? If you don't want to, we'll understand," he said, sweeping his hand around, encompassing the entire orchestra. "However, we want you to be up here with us during this piece."

Caroline looked at Luke, who shook his head. Concern was etched on his face, but Caroline knew escape was not possible. Luke may as well have been a million miles away. She was alone. Her glance fell on Paul, who was oblivious and looked like he was enjoying himself.

EDWARDO TOOK Caroline's elbow and firmly led her back to Grant's piano. He motioned for her to be seated. She reluctantly slid onto the piano bench. Victor Saville was already at the other piano, which faced Caroline's. Edwardo strutted back to the music stand and picked up his baton, signaling the orchestra to get ready. Raising his arms, he brought the baton down sharply, and the orchestra began to play. The music ebbed and flowed for a few minutes, and then Edwardo turned to Victor and nodded. Victor raised his hands above the keys and began to play the first notes of the piece. The concert hall was suddenly graced by beautiful notes, however, the notes were emanating from Caroline's piano. Caroline's fingers danced expertly across the keys and she rocked and swayed with the rhythm. She cocked her head and leaned in toward the keyboard, listening as the mosaic melody poured forth from the depths of the instrument, delighting the thousands of ears and hundreds of souls with otherworldly resonance. When at last she played the final notes of the rendition, she stood and elegantly bowed to Victor and then to the orchestra. The musicians, along with the audience, stood and wildly applauded.

Caroline walked to the stairs where Luke stood waiting to take her hand. He escorted her back to her seat. Calm eventually returned to her after the fourth concerto. Luke held her hand the whole time.

Somewhere in the midst of the music, Paul squeezed Caroline's other hand and whispered, "You've been holding out on me. When and where did you learn to play like that?"

Caroline forced a smile, but didn't answer Paul's question. It certainly was not the time to offer an explanation.

CHAPTER
8

D o I need to be exorcised?" Caroline asked, as she tossed her evening bag onto the table in the foyer. The night's experience was surreal. She didn't know what to think. She turned to Luke, who'd become a rock to her.

Luke stood at the door with his arms folded. It was obvious he was searching for answers of his own. After an awkward pause, he said, "Exorcism is not the answer. We need to convince Grant to leave on his own."

"Oh, don't just stand out there." Caroline held out her hand. "Come on in. I don't want to be alone just yet. Let's go into the kitchen and I'll return the favor and make *you* hot chocolate."

"Something stronger may be in order." Luke said, "I'm so sorry things didn't work out the way we planned."

"That's not your fault. How could we have known?"

"I encouraged you to attend, so, basically, it is my fault."

"Nonsense! Sit down," Caroline ordered, and pointed to a barstool at the kitchen counter. Opening the refrigerator, she said, "I have some white zin, if you'd rather have a glass of wine."

"No, not really, I'm a hot chocolate kind of guy."

"Perfect. You reintroduced me to cocoa. I've found it helps me sleep. Never could stomach the warm milk therapy."

Luke watched Caroline stir the mixture of milk and cocoa. "By the way, when is your birthday?"

"What?" Caroline looked up, "What brought that on?"

"Well, the composition was a birthday gift. I was just wondering."

"Oh, it's in August."

"That encompasses 31 days. Could you narrow it down a bit?"

"August seventeenth. Some birthday present, eh?"

"Well since it's only July, the presents could get better."

"I may not live to see my thirtieth, at this rate, so don't go buying me a Lamborghini."

"Never happen. Don't like the way the doors open. I had something like a Maserati or Ferrari, in mind."

"Forget it! Lamborghini or nothing."

"Okay, nothing works."

After serving the hot chocolate, Caroline sat down at the counter across from Luke. She calmed her shaking hand before lifting her steaming cup to her lips. "Luke, I'm really scared. Tell me what happened up there. I wasn't really present, and I need to know exactly what Grant did through me. What's to keep him from completely taking over my life?"

"We won't let it go that far, and I don't think that is his intention. His main focus is the piano. When Victor hit the first notes, he jerked his head up with an astonished expression on his face. He was shocked to see you playing in unison with him. The entire orchestra looked stunned. Even though they were seeing Grant's widow, they were hearing the man, himself. Edwardo dropped his baton and just stared."

At that moment, the phone jangled, causing both of them to jump.

Caroline arched her eyebrows. "Who could be calling this late?" She picked up the receiver. "Hello?"

"Caroline, hope I didn't wake you," Paul said. "I can't get over how you played this evening. Why didn't you mention to me that you played so well? I feel...deceived, for lack of a better word."

"No, you didn't wake me. I was just having some cocoa. I apologize if you feel I've been deceitful. That was never my intention. I guess I just didn't think it was important. Grant was the musician in the family. I'm just a novice."

"If you're a novice, then so was Liberace!"

"Oh, come on, Paul. It wasn't that good. I picked up a few pointers from Grant. After all, he practiced night-and-day. How could I not absorb some of his technique?" Caroline held up her crossed fingers for Luke to see. He nodded his approval and smiled.

"If you say so. Well, it's late so I'll let you go. Call me if you need anything."

"You know it! Thanks for the call. It's always good to hear from you, and thanks for making the evening so special for me."

Replacing the phone on its cradle, Caroline looked at Luke. "What do you think?"

"You handled it well. I think you may have put him at bay. Back to the matter at hand. I want to confer with a good friend regarding your situation. Amanda Griffith and I went to school together. I've known her almost my entire life. She uses hypnotism, and has read and applied theories attributed to a fifteenth century scholar, Cornelius Agrippa. Agrippa did not adhere to the common belief of that era, that certain individuals possessed secret knowledge capable of unleashing supernatural power. He believed and wrote that magic has nothing to do with sorcery. He contended that magic was nothing more than mind over matter or, in his words, 'Mind over the body.' I've known Amanda to expel spirits from individuals."

"Do you think she could help me?" Caroline asked, with hope in her voice. "After all, Grant isn't just a spirit, I have his blood coursing through my veins, you know. Wouldn't that make a difference?"

Luke looked thoughtful. "That remains to be seen, but it's worth a try. Is that something you would be willing to pursue? If so, I'll arrange a meeting."

"Will you go with me?"

"Absolutely! I'm now involved not only as your psychic, but also as your friend."

Caroline reached across the counter and squeezed Luke's hand with affection. "Thank you so much for that. I'm feeling like a ship lost at sea with a tsunami on the horizon, and no land in sight."

"Don't lose heart—we will find an answer." Luke looked at his watch. "I should go, now. It's been a long, emotional day for us both. Call me, anytime." Luke headed for the door. He looked over his shoulder, "Sure you'll be all right?"

"I think so. I'm so numb. If Grant wants to torment me tonight, he may be in for a disappointment. I don't have the energy to scream, much less respond." Caroline walked Luke to the door. He bent and kissed her gently on the lips. It felt… wonderful. Reluctantly, she let him go.

Luke leaned his cheek against the open door. "Keep smiling—it's not over 'til it's over."

"Sure, easy for you to say. You're not the one who has to face the music."

"And, don't lose that sense of humor. It's part of your charm."

THE NEXT morning, rain pelted the windows, waking Caroline from a drug induced sleep. She had taken two sleeping pills, the night before, to ensure Grant didn't intrude upon her seclusion. She had been taking sleeping pills more often than she liked, but she didn't want to deal with what might happen in her dreams. *Paul will renew my prescription when I run low.*

After taking a shower, she donned her robe and wrapped a towel around her wet hair. Just as she was leaving the bathroom, the phone rang.

"Hello."

"Well, you are alive," Luke responded.

"You sound disappointed."

"Not in the least. Want to have lunch? You slept through breakfast."

"What time is it, anyway?" Caroline asked.

"Eleven."

"Eleven!" Caroline picked up her alarm clock and stared at it. "Ah, sure, give me an hour. I just got out of the shower."

"Can do."

Caroline was ready when Luke arrived to pick her up at noon. On the drive back to the French Quarter, he said, "I called Amanda. She agreed to see you. She is free this afternoon, around three. What do you think?"

"I'm not capable of making decisions, anymore. If you think I should, I will. And, the timing couldn't be more perfect."

"I think you should seize upon the opportunity. What have you got to lose?"

"Then, it's a done deal. Where are we going for lunch?"

"There's a little place on the water called *Freddie's Landing*, specializing in seafood. Sound tempting?"

"Absolutely! I know *Freddie's*. That's one of The Senator's favorite places."

Luke smiled at her. "There's no getting ahead of you, is there?"

"Nope. You may as well just give it up."

"Not a chance. The word 'quitter' is not etched on my family's coat of arms." Luke adjusted the windshield wipers, as the rain increased, "I was hoping it would clear off, so we could sit on the patio, but it's getting worse. Would you rather go somewhere else?"

"No, not at all. My teeth are set for a greasy deep fried Admiral's Platter and a cold mug of beer."

"You read my mind. We're almost there."

When they were seated, and after the waitress took their order, Luke asked, "Did anything unusual happen last night?"

"No, not that I'm aware of," Caroline said, without even blinking. "I took two sleeping pills after you left, and was out like a light. I don't remember a single thing."

"It bothers me that you take so many sleeping pills."

"I'm afraid if I don't, I'll lay awake waiting for Grant's inevitable dreaded appearance. Maybe I'm paranoid, but you know how persistent Grant has been. And, yes, perhaps I should at least cut down on the dosage."

Luke took a sip of beer. "I briefly described to Amanda your dilemma and the troubling aspects of your case. Hopefully, she can ease the situation, somewhat, and get you off the sleeping aids. She told me that, in the past, she had a heart transplant client whom she was able to free from the spirit control of the donor. I'm hopeful she can help you, as well."

"Oh, Luke, if only I could believe this will work. This curse is all consuming. I'm at that point where I'm afraid to even get near a piano. I don't want to be a recluse, but even going out in public is beginning to make me jittery. I never know when Grant is going to show up."

"That's serious. You can't give up your life in order for him to live vicariously through you. We will find an answer, I promise."

"I've always heard promises are made to be broken."

"I've always heard a promise made 'is a debt unpaid.'"

"I guess time will tell!"

A TINY bell above the door tinkled, as Caroline and Luke entered *The Talisman*, a small shop located on Bay Street in the French Quarter. The interior of the shop was bright and clean. Caroline could see a variety of religious objects on the shelves. A glass counter ran the full length of the store and showcased rosaries, crucifixes, prayer books, and other items related to Christian religions. She clung to Luke's arm and tensed, not knowing what to expect. A curtain at the back of the shop parted, and an attractive woman stepped out. Amanda was petite. Her red hair was piled on top her head with strands escaping down the back of her neck. This reminded Caroline of a fad known as "kiss me curls" that the girls wore in high school. Amanda's brown eyes were kind and gentle. Her blue cotton sundress sported an array of yellow sunflowers scattered randomly about. Caroline was immediately drawn to her.

"Amanda, good to see you, again," Luke said, as the two greeted and hugged. Turning to Caroline, he said, "This is Caroline Alexander, the lady I spoke to you about. I hope we're not too early."

"Not at all," Amanda said, extending her hand. Caroline noticed her perfectly manicured nails, as Amanda greeted her. "So nice to meet you."

Caroline said, "Thank you, and I, too, am pleased to meet you. Luke has told me much about you and your skills. I'm very hopeful you will be able to help me."

"I'll certainly try. Come on back to my office where we can have some privacy."

Luke and Caroline followed Amanda into her office.

"Please, make yourselves comfortable," Amanda said.

The room was tastefully appointed. Looking around, Caroline chose one of two brocaded Louis VIII chairs that flanked a beautiful antique marble topped end table. Luke sat in the other one. A turn of the century maroon velvet fainting couch was positioned along one wall.

Amanda slid into the leather chair behind her desk and asked, "Would you like something before we start? Perhaps water or a soda?"

Luke looked at Caroline, who shook her head. "No, thanks. I think we're good."

"Now, Caroline, let me recap what I know from talking to Luke. Approximately five months ago you were given a blood transfusion from your dying husband. After a lengthy hospitalization and recovery, you returned home. Once there, you experienced trance-like encounters with Grant. He talks to you in dreams and tells you he wants you to become a world renowned pianist using your hands. You've told him you didn't want to do this, but he has been relentless and has even made, um, what shall we say, a couple of appearances."

"That's exactly the situation. My hope is you can help me make him understand I don't want to turn my life over to him, and I just want him to leave me alone." Caroline bit her bottom lip. "I don't like saying this, but I'm beginning to dislike him. He can stay the hell out of my life, and I resent him trying to take control of my destiny. Even though it appears he doesn't care what he's doing to me, I do. I won't stand for it!"

"Now that's what I call determination. I do think I can help you. However, let me explain to you my technique. I don't use drugs or exorcism or anything of that nature. I think we can work this through by using what I call 'Mind Over Body.' I will train you how to be strong enough to resist his demands."

Caroline remained resolute. "I hope so! He's determined. He was like that even when he was alive. Everything had to be perfect, and he was obsessed with his quest for perfection."

"Hmm. Once I've taught you how, you'll be able to deter him and take your life back. You'll need to continue to be resolute, though. Persistence overcomes resistance."

"I'm willing to try anything."

"Good! This session is obviously just a consultation. We need to schedule a series of appointments so, once we get started, we can continue without interruption."

Caroline nodded.

Amanda continued, "During these sessions, I will lightly hypnotize you, so that you will be relaxed and receptive to what I'm saying. You may or may not remember exactly what transpires when you come out of hypnosis, but your subconscious will, and you will react automatically when challenges arise."

"Amanda, I'm desperate. How soon can we start?"

Amanda paged through her appointment book. "How about Tuesday, at ten, and then each Tuesday and Thursday, at ten, for—well—for as long as it takes."

"Since I have nothing planned for the rest of my life, because of this curse, that works for me." She broached a look at Luke. "Will you come with me?"

Luke looked at Amanda.

"Of course, Luke is welcome. But, I think you'll find, as we proceed, that you won't need as much outside support."

Luke cleared his throat. "I would like to come once or twice, so I'll rearrange my calendar on those days," he said. "How long are the sessions?"

"One hour. Then, I keep my clients until I'm sure they are completely awake."

"I'll mark off two hours, to be on the safe side."

"Oh, no, Luke," Caroline protested. "How inconsiderate of me. I wasn't thinking. That's too much down time for you, and you have a business to run. I don't want to interrupt your life. I agree with Amanda. I can do this on my own."

Luke responded. "I would like to attend the first couple of sessions, at least—if that is agreeable with the two of you?"

Caroline and Amanda agreed in unison. Caroline smiled at Amanda. She knew she was going to like this woman. Especially if Amanda could rid her of Grant!

CAROLINE TRIED to temper her excited anticipation, as she waited for the next meeting with Amanda. She was full of hope and wouldn't allow herself to become depressed. Finally, it was Tuesday, and she and Luke were back at *The Talisman*.

The threesome exchanged greetings, and once they were situated in Amanda's office, Amanda turned her attention to Caroline.

Softening her voice, she said, "Close your eyes and try not to think of anything. I'm going to put you into a light hypotonic state. When you reach a certain point of relaxation, I will make suggestions, and your mind will be open to receiving them. Remember, I told you that you may or may not remember exactly what transpires when you come out of the hypnosis, but your subconscious will, and you will react automatically, when various situations arise."

Caroline nodded. Luke sat quietly in *his* chair, in the corner of the room.

"Okay, take some deep breaths and clear your thoughts." Amanda approached Caroline and when she touched her, Caroline went limp.

"Caroline, can you hear me?" Amanda said in a subdued voice.

"Yes."

"Good. Listen carefully to what I'm going to tell you. The next time you feel like you're going into a trance, other than here in my office with me, you will resist. You will say out loud, 'I will not allow you to control me. You have no right to disturb my life, and I want you to depart from me.' Now, you repeat those words exactly as I spoke them."

Caroline repeated, "I will not allow you to control me. You have no right to disturb my life, and I want you to depart from me."

"Excellent! Now repeat them, again."

"I will not allow you to control me. You have no right to disturb my life, and I want you to depart from me."

"You're doing great. I'm going to bring you out of the hypnosis. You will feel refreshed and have renewed self-confidence." Amanda snapped her fingers and said, "Wake up, Caroline."

Caroline stirred briefly and slowly sat up. "I remember what you said," she exclaimed with enthusiasm. "Do you really think this will work? I've admonished him before to leave me alone, but he keeps taunting me."

"If you think you can't win, then your subconscious mind will react in that manner. Now you have a new tool to work with. Believe in yourself; that's step number one."

"Thank you, Amanda. I'll try anything to be rid of what I've come to recognize as a curse."

"Even if you have occasion to use it between now and our next appointment, and it works, I want you to come back. We need a few sessions to reinforce your commitment."

"I certainly will. You sound like you're not sure this will work."

"Like I said, it may take a few appointments to cement your resolve. Don't lose faith."

"I'm willing to go the whole nine yards to do whatever it takes to discourage Grant. Keep your fingers crossed, or whatever hypnotists do for good luck."

"Actually, I have a talisman that I wear. You probably didn't realize a Christian cross can be a powerful talisman—you don't need to sprinkle belladonna or throw chicken bones to ward off evil. Quite simply, Caroline, a talisman is an object believed to have magical powers and to cause good things to happen to the person who wears it. It's an object used as a charm to avert evil and bring good fortune and produce miraculous effects. That is according to Webster's. My faith is in the Lord, our God, and I wear the cross to constantly remind me that I am in His hands. And, I strive to follow His direction and to do His will." Amanda pulled her collar back to show Caroline her cross.

"It's beautiful! I want one! I am a believer and I love your theory. Do you sell crosses?"

"No, at least not the ones considered to be fine jewelry. The jewelry store across the street has a wide selection. Tell Sylvia I sent you, and she'll make you a deal. She's a good friend of mine."

"Thank you for your encouragement. I look forward to our next meeting, on Thursday," Caroline said, as she pulled her sneakers on and tied them.

"Looks like we're going to be all right," Amanda said, patting Caroline's shoulder. After Caroline finished tying her shoes, Amanda ushered the two to the front door of the shop and opened it. "The jewelry store is directly across the boulevard," she said. Caroline followed Amanda's pointing finger and saw an upscale store named *Pandora's Jewelry Box*.

"See you Thursday," Luke called back to Amanda, as he took Caroline's elbow and they crossed the street. When they were safely on the other side, he told her, "I like the idea of a talisman, and especially a cross. When I was a kid, I got the daylights scared out of me one Halloween. I was told by some older and, ostensibly, wiser kids that crosses, along with garlic cloves tied around your neck, would stave off vampires. I remember taking mom's favorite and cherished crucifix and her container of Shilling's garlic powder to bed with me that night. In retrospect, I don't recommend the garlic."

Luke opened the door to *Pandora's* and stepped aside, allowing Caroline to enter before him. A very pretty woman came forward from behind a glass counter and greeted them.

"Good afternoon. How may I help you?" she said.

"Good afternoon, Sylvia," Luke responded, noticing the name tag attached to the lapel of her stylish navy blue suit. "We want to see some gold crosses."

"Certainly, we have a wide selection. Please come this way." Sylvia led them to a glass showcase at the back of the shop.

"Yes, that's what we been told. We just came from *The Talisman*." Luke turned and pointed across the street. "Amanda recommended you."

"Ah, yes. Amanda. She's delightful. One of my favorite friends. We go back a long way." Sylvia passed behind the counter, removed a set of keys from her pocket, and opened the glass showcase. She produced a tray covered with blue velvet showcasing an array of crosses with gold chains.

"Hmm, so many to choose from. It's going to be a difficult choice." Luke said, as he turned to Caroline. "Call this an early birthday present, so go ahead and pick the one you like."

"Oh, Luke, I can't let you do that," Caroline said, holding up one of the price tags as she did so.

"Yes, you can." Luke said, wrapping his hand around the proffered tag, hiding it from view. "Don't look at the price. Just pick out the one that inspires you."

"That's easy, I like this one," Caroline said, fingering a simple gold cross with a small peridot gemstone set in the center.

"I like that one, too," Luke said. "And, it's personalized with your birthstone." Luke looked up at Sylvia and nodded. He took a credit card from his wallet and handed it to her.

"Don't bother to wrap it," Caroline said. "I want to wear it."

Sylvia took the cross from the tray and deftly removed the price tag. She handed the cross to Caroline and looked at Luke. "I give Amanda's friends a twenty-five percent discount. I'll be right back with your receipt."

"Thank you, Sylvia, but that's not necessary."

"I know," Sylvia said, as she walked toward the cash register at the front of the store. "Luke, will you please help me?" Caroline asked, lifting her hair with both hands so Luke could fasten the clasp at the back of her neck.

"My pleasure," he said, as he fumbled with the small C-ring clasp.

As soon as Luke had the cross secured, Sylvia was back with the credit card receipt for him to sign. He scribbled his name across the bottom.

"The piece has a lifetime guarantee," Sylvia said, handing Luke a copy of the receipt. "If it gets damaged in any way, bring it back, and we'll fix it or replace it."

"Can't beat a deal like that," Luke said, as he slid the receipt and guarantee in his shirt pocket.

Caroline lovingly caressed the cross, as the trio made their way to the exit. She looked at Luke and said, "Thank you so much."

Luke's warm smile showered her with affection. "You're more than welcome." He held the door open.

"It's been a pleasure to serve you," Sylvia said, extending her hand toward Luke.

Luke took her hand, "Thanks for your help, Sylvia. Hopefully, this is just what the doctor ordered."

Once outside, Caroline said, "Luke, this is a very special gift. Every time I wear it, which will be all the time, I will think of you."

"Hopefully, it will be a fond remembrance."

"Why? Are you thinking of deserting me?" Anxiety crept into Caroline's voice.

"No! Never! I meant something to remember me by when we're not together."

"Oh, that's different. I don't really need a reminder, but the sentiment is sweet." Caroline caressed her cross again and said, "We should go by the church on our way home and have the priest bless this. Extra help couldn't hurt."

"Good idea."

"I know where there's a church near here. Holy Trinity. It's within walking distance," Caroline said. "I, well, that is my sorority sisters and I, used to go there and attend Mass on Sunday, after a night of drinking and debauchery. Maybe the priest will recognize me, if he's still there." After a brief pause, she added, "On second thought, maybe that isn't such a good idea."

Luke raised his eyebrows.

"Oh, don't look so shocked, I'm just kidding. We didn't drink that much."

"I see. Just engaged in debauchery?"

"Wouldn't you like to know?" Caroline teased.

"Come on," Luke said, taking her by the hand. "I know everything. Remember what I do for a living."

Caroline blushed. "Thank you, again, for the talisman, Luke. You give me hope in so many ways. I could never thank you enough."

"You already have. And now, you have two lucky charms, the cross and, of course, me!"

THE CHURCH was almost deserted when they arrived. A few pilgrims dotted the pews, in somber contemplation, as the couple entered the dim and cool interior. A rack of votive candles stood against one wall, directly inside the entrance. The candles' flames danced in the shadows, as the gentle breeze from the open door toyed with them. All the candles were lit, Caroline surmised, due to the Lenten season.

She was instantly encircled in a peace she remembered from a time before Grant's untimely demise. Noticing the holy water receptacles were empty, Caroline headed to the front pew and knelt before the altar, making the sign of the cross. She felt Luke kneel beside her, and was comforted by his presence. She bowed her head and prayed.

Gracious, merciful and heavenly Father please look with kindness upon the petition of your humble servant. I come before You and ask forgiveness for my many sins and plead that You grant me that forgiveness and give me peace. I live in constant torment and beg that, if it be Your will, You lift this curse from me. I also pray that You take Grant into Your loving arms and bestow upon him peace, as well. He apparently is also tormented. Thank You for all the blessings You have bestowed on me. I know all good things come from You.

When she looked up, a priest stood in front of her. "I didn't want to disturb your prayer, young lady, but I wanted to welcome you back to Holy Trinity. I haven't seen you at Mass for quite some time."

Caroline recognized the frail, elderly holy man wearing a traditional black cassock and white collar. His hair was completely white, but his bright gray eyes were still vivid and probing.

"Father Jonathan! How nice to see you!" Caroline judged by the age lines and the priest's bent posture that she had been away from Holy Trinity longer than she realized.

"You looked as though you were praying hard. I've been standing here for several minutes."

"Yes. I was." Caroline introduced her companion. "Father, this is a friend of mine, Quinton Lucas."

The priest extended his hand. "Pleased to meet you, Quinton."

"Thank you, Father. Please, call me Luke."

"All right, Luke it is. I haven't seen you here before."

"That's right. I attend church over by Jackson Square."

"Ah, yes. Father Murphy's bailiwick. He's a fine fellow. We lunch together at least once a week, and exchange war stories." Quickly adding, "Nothing confidential, that is."

"That would go without saying, Father. And, I agree, Father Murphy is good man." Luke hesitated a moment before saying, "We have a favor to ask of you, Father."

"Sure, what is it?"

"I would like for you to bless my cross," Caroline interjected, and held her new cross up for the priest to see.

"Why, of course! Come on back to the baptismal. It's the only holy water available, right now. The other vessels are being cleaned after all of the Lenten observances."

As they gathered around the fountain, Father Jonathan gingerly reached for the cross still fastened on the gold chain around Caroline's neck.

"Ouch," he cried. "I just got shocked." He instinctively stepped back.

"What happened?" Caroline was stunned.

Disguising his embarrassment, the priest said, "Oh, nothing. Probably static electricity. Let's try that, again." He tentatively reached for the cross. This time he was able to complete the ritual without incident.

After the blessing, Caroline said, "Thank you, Father. It's good to see you, again."

"You're welcome, my child. Don't be a stranger." The priest blessed her with the sign of the cross, and then added, "Our door is always open. Now, go in peace, to love and serve the Lord."

"Good day, Father," Caroline said. "Thank you, again, for the blessing. May God continue to favor you, for all you do." She started toward the exit, but turned back in time to see Luke hand the priest a twenty dollar bill.

"No need for that."

"I want to, Father. Thank you. It means a lot to Caroline for you to bless her cross, and…"

Luke lowered his voice, and Caroline couldn't hear what he said to the priest, who seemed concerned and said something back to Luke. Upon his reply, the priest nodded emphatically. She wondered what Luke had said to elicit such a response. When he joined her, she asked.

"I just asked him to pray for you."

When they reached the double mahogany doors, Caroline waved to Father Jonathon, who waved back. His reedy voice echoed in the chamber. "May His peace be with you, always."

I pray for that constantly, thought Caroline, as the two made their way into the late afternoon air.

ONCE OUTSIDE the church, Caroline whispered, "Luke, what do you think that was all about?"

"What?"

"When Fr. Jonathan touched the cross."

"Oh, that. I suspect it was just like he said, static electricity."

"I'm not so sure."

"Come on, now. You don't think Grant has—"

"No, of course not," Caroline replied. She felt foolish and a little embarrassed.

As they approached Luke's vehicle, he said, "Hey, do you like football?"

"How can you live in New Orleans and not like football? Love the Saints."

"Well, it just so happens the Saints have an exhibition game this afternoon, and yours truly has a couple of tickets. Wanna go?"

"Are you kidding?" Caroline punched his arm. "How long you been holding out on me?"

"I take that as a yes."

"YES! Yes, I wanna go. What time?"

"We have exactly forty eight minutes.

"Well, we're burnin' daylight, partner. Let's hitch up and skedaddle outta here."

"I'm all over it," Luke said, putting the Rover in gear.

THE COUPLE claimed their seats just as the announcer asked the attendees to stand for the playing of the National Anthem. The fans stood facing the American flag and placed their right hands over their hearts. When the music began, Caroline violently jerked and looked up at Luke. She wasn't hearing *The Star Spangled Banner*, she was hearing *Turn Back to Me*! She tugged on Luke's arm to get his attention. He looked down at her and smiled before returning his gaze to the flag. *He isn't hearing the same song as I. What the hell? Everyone is hearing the anthem but me.*

At the conclusion of the playing and amid the riotous cheering and applause, Caroline sat down onto the bleacher. Luke took his seat. "How 'bout a hotdog and a beer?" he asked. Then, "Whoa, Caroline, what's wrong? You look like you've seen a—oh, don't tell me."

She looked up, miserable. "I didn't hear the anthem. The song I heard was *Turn Back to Me*. Grant even controls what I'm hearing now."

Luke slouched next to her, shoulder to shoulder. "I don't know what to say. Do you want to leave?"

Caroline thought about it, but then she stuck out her chin. "Hell, no! He's not going to get away with it. I'll fight him with everything I have." After a slight pause, she added, "And, yes, I'd love a hotdog and a beer."

Luke put his arm around her and hugged her close, "That's my girl. I'll be right back. Don't go away."

"Not a chance."

After the game, on their way to the parking lot, Luke asked, "Do you want to go home or stay with me a little longer?"

"I talk a braver game than I feel. If you don't mind, I'd like to stay with you a little longer."

"That works for me, too."

Back at Luke's place, Luke prepared a dinner of baked cod and roasted Brussel sprouts. After eating and cleaning the mess, they lounged in the living room. Luke put some soft music on, and Caroline finally felt relaxed.

"Do you remember what Amanda told me to say?"

"Yes. Luke said, "I remember every word. 'You will say out loud, *I will not allow you to control me. You have no right to disturb my life and I want you to depart from me.*"

"Good. Let's try it if you're up to it, Luke. I'm feeling stronger and more like I can face him down. Will you try to contact him?"

"I will."

Luke leaned back and sunk into the sofa. Caroline sat across from him, watching. His eyes closed and he began breathing more slowly.

Moments later, Caroline heard Grant's voice coming from Luke.

"Caroline… "

"NO! Grant, leave me alone! I will not allow you to control me! You have no right to disturb my life and I want you to depart from me. I do not want to hear what you have to say, so don't even speak to me."

"Darling, you can't shut me out that easily. Ultimately, you will see things my way. Quit trying to resist, you know you can't win. How often do I have to prove that to you?"

"You're wrong! I can win and will win. I will find a way! I do not intend to live the rest of my life for you!"

"We'll see, Caroline. We'll see."

"Yes, Grant! We'll see." Caroline defiantly crossed her arms. She watched Luke gradually came out of the trance.

Running his hands through his hair, he said, "I heard. I wondered if you'd forgotten Amanda's direction."

"No, well, perhaps. I was so angry I just couldn't control myself. Did I spoil it?"

"I don't think so. You really gave him an ear full. Don't give up. You cannot let him wear you down."

"I'm already worn down, Luke."

"I remember what an old parish priest once told me, 'If God be with you, who can be against you?'"

"I know that verse. I've heard it all my life. But, where's God, now? If Grant can hide car keys and slam the keyboard lid down, what else is he capable of doing? So far, nothing has worked." Caroline paused, "I feel like I'm imposing on you. Maybe I should go home."

"And, how will you be better off at home—alone?"

"Oh, I don't know. I don't know anything, anymore. There was a time when even if I was wrong, I was not in doubt."

"I want you to stay, but it's up to you."

Caroline nodded her head and went to where Luke sat. She snuggled next to him and placed her head firmly on his shoulder. Luke pulled her into him and kissed her sweetly on the lips. She responded and put her arms around his neck. He held her close.

"I'm here for you, always will be," he whispered.

She hugged him tightly and said, "Always is a long time. I'm not even sure I have tomorrow. To borrow a thought from one of my favorite songs, *Don't give me tomorrow, take me day-by-day. Don't add to my sorrow…*"

CHAPTER

9

After falling asleep, that night, Caroline was awakened by a violent thunderstorm. Jagged bolts of white light rent the night air, and the following booms shook Caroline's windows. She sat upright and looked at the clock on her nightstand. 1:17 a.m.

Damn it, I'll never get back to sleep, I should have taken two sleeping pills. She threw back the sheets and went to the bathroom. Caroline always kept a nightlight on. Even when she was married, she could not tolerate complete darkness. In the current state of affairs, her fetish had grown worse, but with the storm, she was even more anxious. She looked at her image in the mirror. Dark circles had smudged her eyes, and no amount of concealer had diminished the haunted look they had taken on. She picked up a brush and was about to run it through her disheveled mane, when the hair on the back of her neck began to rise. She looked furtively behind her and then dashed to the door, slamming it shut.

Leaning against it, she prayed. *Please, God. In your goodness and mercy, give Grant peace, so he can be content in the afterlife. Please, I beseech you.*

Just as her prayer ended, the nightlight sputtered out. Caroline dared not move in the intense darkness. Gasping, she threw out a hand until it touched the wall. Her fingers frantically searched for the light switch and she cried out, as she flipped it on. Nothing. She toggled it up and down. Still nothing. Fear slithered up from her gut and emerged in a long groan. Clapping a hand over her mouth, she calculated the risk of leaving the bathroom, and finally found a sliver of courage. She quietly opened the door and edged herself out. The first thing she looked at was her clock. No numbers illuminated from its face. *The power must have gone out.* For an instant she felt like laughing, but she was afraid she wouldn't be able to stop. Dashing to the window, she saw the street lights were out, too. Maybe the whole city was dark. A huge sigh escaped her. *Nothing spooky here, folks. Go back to bed.*

She picked up the telephone receiver, but found the phone was also dead. In her mind, she could see her cell phone charging on the kitchen counter. She shook her head. *There is no way I'm wandering this dark house to get it!*

Not knowing what else to do, Caroline returned to her bed. She curled up and pulled the coverlet up around her shoulders. As the rain pelted her windows and the night sky reverberated, she finally drifted off to sleep.

CAROLINE, THE hypnotism will not free you from me. I'm the only one who can do that and I'm not inclined to do so. You must quit fighting me. You will do as I say because you have no choice. Didn't I prove that at the symphony? No one can help you. You have no choice.

A CACOPHONY of birds chirping woke Caroline the next morning. Raindrops glistened on the window panes, while ravaged leaves clung to the wetness. Caroline sat up and stretched. She noticed the clock was lit, and she could see the bathroom light was on. She wondered when the electricity had been restored. She moved to get up, and then she remembered the dream.

She sank back onto the mattress, not sure if she would explode or implode. He wasn't going to stop! She remembered how headstrong Grant was when he'd been alive. It was his way or no way. Always. She shook her head. When had she gotten so wimpy? Where had that troublemaking student gone? The one who took no crap from anyone. She'd been so angry growing up, she'd embraced it in order to survive. And yet, when she'd married Grant, it had gone away. Well…maybe it hadn't gone away. Maybe Grant had stomped it out with the sheer strength of his ego. However it happened, somewhere along the way, she had lost herself.

"Grant, I'm not going to let you rob me of my future. And…and I'll say it out loud…I'm glad you are gone! You hear me? Glad! You bastard, you ruled me while you lived, but I'm not going to let you do it after you've died. I'll find a way. Believe me. Do you hear me?"

Caroline realized she was screaming. She choked her next words off and smoothed out the covers that she'd crumpled in her lap. Whispering, she said, "I'll find a way."

Downstairs, Caroline heard the piano keyboard lid slam down. With shaky hands, she picked up the phone and punched in Luke's number. Throwing a wary glance towards the bedroom door, she ran into the bathroom and locked the door.

"'Lo," came a sleepy voice at the other end of the line.

"Luke, I'm so sorry to wake you."

"Caroline, what's happened?"

"He's here. He came to me in my sleep and just now, he slammed the lid on the piano. I'm scared, Luke."

"I'm on my way. Where are you, now?"

"Locked in the bathroom—like that's going to deter him. He knows about Amanda and told me the hypnotism wouldn't work. He said he was the only one who could free me from his grasp. Oh, Luke, I wish I'd been the one to die!"

"Caroline, don't talk like that. Stay where you are. I'll honk three times when I'm in the driveway, so you can let me in. Twenty minutes, tops."

"Okay," came her weak reply.

CAROLINE SLID down the door and sat on the bathroom floor with her arms wrapped around her knees. After about twenty minutes she heard three honks coming from the driveway. She ran down the stairs, wrenched the front door open and lunged into Luke's arms.

"Oh, Luke, I've been so upset. Thank you for coming."

"Shhh, just relax. Come on outside. The air is fresh after the rain. Let's sit on the patio for a while, and you can tell me all about it."

"Did you get a storm, last night? It thundered and rained like hell here. It woke me up, and after the electricity went off, I got scared and hid under the covers. I don't know when I fell asleep, but he came to me, again."

"What happened? What did he say?"

Caroline laid her head on Luke's shoulder, and he pulled her close to him. For the first time in a long time, she felt safe. She snuggled even closer.

"He said the hypnotism would not work, and he was the only one who could free me from his control!" Caroline sat up straight. "Do you think it's true?"

"I'm sure he wants you to think that all is hopeless, so you won't pursue any other avenue. Since you asked my opinion, I'll tell you. I think he's a bully, and like all bullies, they really are weak. My thinking is he's scared. You're obviously not the quiet little mouse he'd been married to, and he's trying to intimidate you. I say let's move forward in our plan, in spite of his threats. Time will tell, but I have a feeling he's not going to be the one standing at the end of this."

"Luke, I'm a train wreck. I don't know what to do or where to turn. I feel like I keep grasping at straws. I'm afraid to stay here, alone. This, damn it, is my home and I'm afraid to stay here." She turned to face him. "May I stay with you for a few days? I feel very vulnerable, and I'm even wondering how I'm going back into that house, much less sleep there. I promise not to be a bother."

"Of course, you're welcome to stay with me. Together, we may be able to convince him his scheme will not work."

"You really think so?"

"Come on. Let's check out the house, and then you can pack some things. Luke led Caroline through the French doors into the house. "Let's check out that piano, first."

They stepped into the drawing room, hand in hand; Caroline reluctantly. "It's okay," Luke said, and headed to the piano. He examined the lid, lifting it and peering under it. After replacing it, he stepped back and circled the piano, looking for anything that could explain the lid slamming down. He finally said, "I'm feeling a lot of energy coming through, this morning. I want to try to contact Grant, right now. I feel his presence."

"I'm not sure; I'm pretty shaken from last night."

"With me here, you need not fear. What do you say?"

"Well, all right." Caroline sat on the sofa and tucked her legs up under her. She grabbed the throw and wrapped it around her. If she could, she'd hide under it, but she didn't want Luke—and certainly not Grant—to know how really scared she was.

Luke sat down at the piano and lifting the lid to the keyboard, he put his hands lightly on the keys. A second later, he jerked them away, just before the cover slammed down. Caroline screamed and jumped up. Luke caught her, as she reached the stairs.

"Caroline! No, don't go. Come back."

She slowly turned. Luke gathered her into his arms. "Don't be afraid. It's all going to be okay. I promise."

"I can't. I just can't take any more of this torture."

She screamed, again, when Grant's voice began to speak into her ear. She pushed Luke away, and his head fell back.

"Caroline, you silly girl. It is not my intent to torture you. You're being ridiculous by refusing to grant me my wish. What possible harm could come to you from simply playing the piano? If you don't capitulate—well, let's just say, I have other means of convincing you."

Caroline stepped back and shouted, "How dare you threaten me! You can't really hurt me! You're a spirit. I want you to stop, right now. Grant, can't you understand. I don't want to spend my life living *your* dream. Can't you see how this is affecting me? Don't you care? Ha! Of course, you don't. You didn't while alive, so why should you be any different dead? You're driving me mad."

"Caroline, just stop that nonsense! Many people would jump at a chance to do what I'm asking of you."

"Of course, it's just like you to think that everyone would like to be you! Well, here's a newsflash. I'm not *many people*. Why don't you go find someone else to do your bidding?"

"Ah, but don't you see, you have my blood."

Caroline raised her hand and slapped Luke's face, successfully shutting that horrible voice up, and bringing Luke out of the trance. He shook his head.

"What the hell was that? Did you strike me?"

"Yes. No. Well, I didn't strike you, exactly. I took a swing at Grant, and your face just happened to be in the way."

"Oh." Luke rubbed his jaw. "I felt Grant leave, as soon as you, er, hit me. Nice right hook, by the way. Apparently," he smiled, "Grant can dish it out, but can't take it."

"I'm not a boxer, Luke!" Her laugh was a bit hysterical. "Sorry about that." She reached out and touched Luke's cheek, which was reddening up, fast. "Yeah, he was like that when he was alive, too. How much do you remember of his diatribe?"

"Everything. I wasn't completely under. Remember, I asked you because I wanted him to come through, and he took advantage of the opportunity."

Caroline clenched her fists and asked, "Can I get a complete blood replacement and rid myself of this curse?"

"You're joking, of course?"

"NO! Can that be done?"

"No, it cannot. And, getting different blood would not solve the problem. His characteristics are now embedded in your cells. I suggest you proceed with Amanda. Grant may be trying to dissuade you from following through because he may fear it could work. What do you think?"

"I'm too emotional and too tired. I can't think and I'm not capable of making decisions. I'm giving you the keys to this bus. You drive for a while." She gripped his shoulders and shook him. "Please!"

"Whoa, don't slug me, again." He softened his words with a wink. "Let's at least give Amanda a try. Go put some things together for a few days," Luke said, turning Caroline toward the stairs.

Caroline took a few steps, and then turned. "I should call Paul and tell him I'm going to be gone, so he won't send the militia out to find me."

"I agree. Can I help you get ready?"

"No, just stay close. This won't take long."

CAROLINE DIALED Paul's number, and he picked up on the first ring.

"Caroline, I was just thinking about you. Is everything all right?"

"Yes, all's well. I'm calling to let you know I'm going to be gone a few days and didn't want you to worry about me."

Paul did not respond.

"You still there?" Caroline asked.

"Yes, I'm here. This is sudden. Where are you going?"

Caroline contrived an answer. "Well, you see, Marcella, an old college buddy called and invited me to come for a visit. She lives in the Keys."

"Um, the Keys." Caroline heard suspicion in his voice.

"It'll be good to get away, relax, and relive the wild and wooly college days with an old friend."

"You should give me a contact, in case The Senator tries to reach you."

"Dad has my cell phone number and can reach me, anytime."

"Well, I really don't like the way this sounds, Caroline. You're just up and leaving on the spur of the moment? Come on, what's going on?"

"You're always suspicious of my motives, Paul. Nothing is going on. Marcella telephoned a few days ago and invited me. At first, I declined, but the more I thought of it, the more I liked it. The Keys have always intrigued me, so I called her back and accepted her invitation. She promised a relaxing atmosphere and great seafood. Now, tell me, how could I resist?"

"Still…"

"There you go, putting restraints on me. I'm a grown woman, almost thirty years old, and capable of making decisions of my own. I'll be in touch, don't worry about me."

"Okay, since you put it that way. Make sure you call me, daily."

"Daily? Maybe not, but I'll keep in touch. Take care, Paul. Bye." Caroline hung up, before Paul could protest. She rolled her eyes at Luke. Luke gave her thumbs up.

ONCE THEY arrived at Luke's apartment, Luke deposited Caroline's luggage in the guest room.

"This is beginning to feel more like home than my own home. I can't begin to thank you enough for everything you've done. You've been like a guardian angel."

"That's quite a comparison, but totally unwarranted. I feel guilty over the incident at the symphony.

If I hadn't encouraged you to go, the unpleasant events would never have occurred."

"Don't beat yourself up too much over that. Apparently, Grant is going to insert himself into my life regardless of where I am or what I'm doing. I may be counting too much on Amanda."

"Amanda is just one avenue to explore. If that doesn't work, well, back to the drawing board."

By the time the couple arrived at Luke's, it was late afternoon. They hadn't had breakfast or lunch so Luke said, "It's a bit early, but I'm hungry. Do you want to go out, or take a chance on my cooking, again?"

"So far, the food's been great, so why don't we make dinner together? I used to be a good cook but, having been away from it for so many months, I can't guarantee the results."

"Singularly, we fail. Together we succeed, sweetie. Anyway, if we fail, there's always McDonald's."

"Since you're confident enough for the both of us, I'll follow your lead. Just give me an apron and directions."

Luke pulled food items from the refrigerator. "I think we'll have grilled salmon with a shrimp or two, tossed in for variety, accompanied by a baked potato. I'm going to leave you in charge of the salad, while I start the grill. You okay with that?"

"Damn straight. I'm the salad wizard. I'll set the table, too."

"Looks like we got the bases covered. Back in a few."

Caroline hummed a tune, as she rinsed the Iceberg lettuce and two tomatoes. She rummaged around in the refrigerator and found a cucumber and a red bell pepper to add to the mix. She scrounged around in the cabinet where the seasonings were stored looking for ingredients so she could make the dressing herself. *Trying to impress your host?* She smiled. Maybe she was.

It suddenly dawned on her how content she was in Luke's kitchen. The guy generated confidence in her, and she felt safe in his company. She also recognized that she was beginning to have feelings for him. *Is it too soon? What would The Senator think about her jumping into a romance, just months after Grant's death?* She knew he probably wouldn't like it, for whatever reason. *What is it about the men in my life? Dad, Grant, Paul…none of them seem to want me happy!* As she tore the drained lettuce, she thought of Luke. He was the only one who genuinely cared that she was okay. He was someone worth holding on to. She remembered his words to her earlier. He'd called her "sweetie." She felt her cheeks grow hot, as she tossed the salad together.

Who was she kidding? *Getting romantically involved at this point in my life would only add more confusion, and I'm already running on empty. If, and when, the Grant issue is resolved, I can contemplate the future. Right now, I wonder if I even have a future. I need to put my heart on hold—at least for now.*

Caroline sensed Luke's eyes on her while they ate. She glanced up, and yes, he was gazing at her with a combination of admiration, curiosity, and something else that Caroline couldn't quite identify. Trepidation, maybe? They said little during the meal, and when they spoke, it was about things that really didn't matter. Caroline felt something deep was transpiring, on a subconscious level, and she was just along for the ride. In between trite words, she wanted to tell him how important he'd become to her. She wanted to ask if he'd be willing to wait on her heart until everything with Grant was buried. Caroline wasn't sure her heart was in full agreement with her decision to put her feelings on hold. After all, hearts have a mind of their own.

AFTER DINNER and dishes, Luke suggested they take a stroll and enjoy the coolness of the evening.

"Sounds like we're thinking the same thing. There's always something going on in Jackson Square," Caroline said, as she pulled on a sweater. "Want to go explore?"

The couple walked hand-in-hand through the streets of the French Quarter and stopped several times to chat with the venders who had their booths set up along the bustling boulevard. The never-ending supply of amusement seekers was a force to be reckoned with, even on the so-called off nights when there was no apparent cause for celebration. The French Quarter was alive and well.

"Look, Luke. There's a gypsy fortune teller," Caroline said, pulling Luke toward the booth occupied by a rather mysterious-looking woman. Her face was so gaunt, she looked as though she was living on borrowed time. The booth consisted of a card table covered with a soft black velvet cloth and two folding chairs, positioned across from the vendor. The gypsy's eyes were deeply sunken, but immediately engaged anyone who happened to glance her way. She blithely shuffled her deck of tarot cards, but when she caught Caroline's eye, she beckoned to her with a crooked forefinger.

"Oh, look, Luke. She wants to read my cards. Do you mind?"

"Caroline, you know that's rubbish."

However, Caroline had already seated herself at the table. The gypsy's smile exposed yellowed irregular teeth punctuated by a few gaps. Smiling back, Caroline banished the memory of the museum mummy she'd seen as a child.

A simple reading was ten dollars, the placard on the table said. Caroline patted her side, and then remembered she hadn't brought her handbag.

"Please, Luke, just for fun." She held out her hand, and Luke reluctantly passed her a ten dollar bill. She held it out to the gypsy.

"Just for fun, huh?"

After lifting the bill to the light and checking for its authenticity, the gypsy slipped it quickly into the folds of her ample bosom. Her armful of bangles jingled, as she did so. After securing the payment, the gypsy slowly pushed the deck of tarot cards toward Caroline indicating she should cut them. The gypsy took little heed of Luke, as he sat in the chair beside Caroline. He watched intently. The gypsy began turning the cards over, one by one, explaining the meaning of each as she placed them in expert alignment on the table in front of her.

THE GYPSY tapped the first card with her knurled forefinger, and began the reading.

"*The Fool* indicates beginnings, journeys or a new life cycle which can be mental, physical, or spiritual," she said. "Also, *The Fool* controls over-turning or disturbing your current state by unexpected happenings." Hesitating for a moment, she continued, "Some very important decisions are to be made."

Caroline grabbed Luke's hand so tightly he winced. "She knows," Caroline whispered in Luke's ear.

He shook his head and whispered back. "That could apply to almost everyone, Caroline. Take it easy. Are you sure you want to continue?"

"Yes!" Looking at the gypsy, Caroline begged, "Please, go on."

The gypsy gave Luke a look of disdain, as she turned over the second card.

"Ah! *The Star*." Caroline detected a sparkle in the gypsy's eyes. "I see you are experiencing some self-doubt? *The Star* shows that you have an unwillingness to change and accept new opportunities that may present themselves. Also, there is an inability to express yourself freely. Something or someone seems to be controlling you." She looked at Caroline with raised eyebrows, apparently expecting some reaction.

Luke felt Caroline stiffen. They both sat silently, waiting for the next revelation. The gypsy, releasing her gaze from Caroline, slowly turned over the third card, *Judgment*.

"This card denotes stagnation and delay in action. Do you have a fear of change or even a fear of death in your current state? I'm sensing loss and separation has recently affected your life. Am I right?"

Luke put a hand on Caroline's. "I've had enough, Caroline. Let's move on." He tugged at her arm.

"No! I need to know what the cards have in store," Caroline said, pushing Luke's hand away. "This may help me cope with, you know, with Grant."

The gypsy arched her eyebrows waiting for Caroline's next move. She ignored Luke.

"Go on," Caroline ordered.

When the gypsy turned over the fourth card, Caroline and Luke both flinched when they saw it. It was *Death*.

"HO, HO! Not to be so jumpy," the gypsy warned. "The *Death* card is not as drastic as you may think. In fact, it designates the beginning of a new life, transformation and change—major changes. It signifies the end of a phase which has served its purpose. Due to past events, there may be an abrupt change in life patterns and behavior."

Luke put his arm around Caroline's shoulders and pulled her close. The gypsy turned over the next card. Lifting her eyes, she fixed her gaze on Caroline.

She said in almost a scolding tone, "You have a very interesting reading, my dear. *The Magician* shows confusion and an inability to make choices. Appears you have talents you will not use and talents you are willing to give up easily. You don't recognize your potential and lack the power to initiate." The gypsy hesitated before turning over the next card and peered at Caroline as if waiting for permission to do so.

"Go on," Caroline pleaded. She hung tightly to Luke's arm.

The gypsy retrieved the next card from the deck and turned it over. "Ah, yes, *The Three of Wands.* This card indicates imprisonment. Drastic change that takes away freedom of expression."

The gypsy turned over the fifth card, *The Chariot.*

"This card designates disregard for others and envy. Chaos in your personal life, imbalance and destruction. Also, there is a warning against over-whelming ambition."

"How many cards constitute a reading?" Luke growled.

"Oh, usually seven, unless the patron wants to continue with more."

Luke turned to Caroline. "Is there any point in looking at the next two cards?"

"Yes, we've gone this far," Caroline replied, and waived her hand for the gypsy to continue.

"As you wish, my dear," the gypsy turned over the sixth card.

"*The Hanged Man*." The gypsy tapped the card with her long fingernail. "There is a failure to act with an inability toward progress."

She paused waiting for a reaction and when none was forthcoming, she leaned back in her chair and slid the seventh and last card from the deck. It was *The Tower.*

Luke breathed a sigh of relief. At last it was almost over. Caroline held her breath, fearing the worst card would be the last. She was not disappointed.

"I see drastic change robbing you of your freedom of expression. This could be financial disaster or even imprisonment. There are sudden changes out of your control, an overthrow of an existing way of life. Ruin and upheaval. There could be imprisonment situated in some circumstances which you cannot alter or control at present."

"Okay, that rips it. Let's go," Luke knocked his chair over, as he leapt up. "This is ridiculous. This— this woman is a shyster!"

"Luke, please wait. I want to talk to her. Maybe she can give me some insight about what I should do. So far no one else has been able to provide me with a solution."

"Are you serious? This has been way over the top. I'm taking you home." Luke firmly gripped Caroline's arm and forced her to her feet.

"What are you doing? I'm running out of hope, and she may be able to give me some answers!"

"After that reading, what kind of answers are you expecting? 'Oh, my dear, you must surrender to the force that is trying to control you, otherwise you will never have peace.'" Luke jammed his hands into his pants pockets and stalked off into the night. Caroline raced after him.

"I'm sorry, Luke. I'm just so desperate. Can't you understand? Please don't turn your back on me. I need you."

Luke turned to face her, and Caroline fell into his embrace. He held her tightly, and she clung to him. After a moment, he gently separated and guided her back to his apartment. Caroline felt like a rag doll, all energy drained with each card that had been turned. After locking the door, Luke led Caroline to his bedroom where he gently undressed her. He took a clean Saints T-shirt from his dresser drawer and slipped in on over her head. Then he pointed to the bed. She took the hint and lay down. He curled up beside her and enfolded her in his embrace. Caroline snuggled into his chest and wept. After a while, her tears subsided and she sniffed.

"I got your shirt all wet. I'm sorry."

"It's no problem. I kind of like it."

"What an accommodating man you are." Caroline laid her head on his chest and fell asleep.

"WELL, GOOD morning, Sleepy Head." Caroline self-consciously pulled down the T-shirt Luke had dressed her in the night before and continued making breakfast.

Luke sidled up to her and kissed her forehead. "Nice legs!" he said, grabbing a grape from a bowl and tossing it into his mouth. He held one up to Caroline's lips. "You had me scared. How are you doing, today?"

Caroline replied, "I'm okay. I relived our session with the gypsy, and you're absolutely right, the reading could apply to ninety percent of the population. It was just too personal at the time to ignore. Thank you for your discretion and for insulating me from further anxiety."

Slipping back into his John Wayne camouflage, Luke answered, "Why, you're welcome, Purdy Lady. Saving damsels in distress is my mission."

"Okay, *partner*, add another notch to your belt. You saved me." Caroline nudged her savior away from the counter and popped two slices of bread in the toaster. "How does the Duke like his eggs? His choices are scrambled or scrambled."

"Know what, scrambled sounds good. What can I do to help?" Luke eyed the countertop, which was set with plates, silver service, and orange juice in two sparkling glasses.

"Got it under control. Go wash. This is your two minute warning."

"I'm on it!"

After breakfast, Caroline said, "I need to do some shopping, but don't have my car."

"That isn't a problem. You can drop me off at my office and use the Range Rover the rest of the day. My last appointment ends at four, so you can pick me up, about then. You know where my parking space is."

"Yes, I do, and that's very nice of you. Do you need anything while I'm out-and-about?"

"Hmm, nothing I can think of. I have a freezer full of food. We could barricade ourselves for over six months and not starve. However, perishables need to be replenished; milk, fresh fruit and vegetables, and the like."

"I can do that."

"Deal. We need to hustle; I have a ten o'clock. You have my number if you need me for anything."

Caroline smiled at Luke. "Why, Luke, I do believe you like me." She was pleased to see his face redden.

After dropping Luke off at his office, Caroline went to the shopping center. As she was choosing fresh vegetables and placing them in her shopping cart, she felt someone touch her elbow. Turning, Caroline almost bumped into the gypsy fortune teller, who was standing behind her.

"Oh, my. You startled me," Caroline said, clutching her sweater.

"I'm sorry. I didn't mean to. I didn't remember your name and wanted to get your attention."

"Why?" Caroline instinctively knew the answer before she asked the question.

"We didn't get to finish your reading and there is something you should know."

Caroline blanched. "Oh, no. Is it bad news?"

"Depends." The gypsy moved closer. Caroline shuddered, not knowing what she was about to hear.

"The fellow that was with you, is his name Grant?" the gypsy asked.

Caroline held onto the shopping cart for support. After a few seconds, she managed to say, "No, why?"

The gypsy moved closer still. Caroline winced. The gypsy seemed oblivious to Caroline's reaction. She said, "Sometimes I channel, although I'm not a dedicated medium. That could be because of what I do, you know, fortune telling. Anyone can be a channel."

"Yes, yes. Go on," Caroline wished she'd just spit it out!

"Well, I sensed that all during the reading someone was trying to come through. He called himself Grant. Do you know a Grant?"

Why am I not surprised? Now he's channeling through other people to get to me. "Ah, yes. He was my husband. He was killed several months ago, in an auto accident. What did he want?"

"His message was simple. He kept saying, 'You won't win, give it up. You have no choice.'" The gypsy exposed a stained and gap-toothed smile. "Are you all right?" she asked.

"Yes. I'm just fine. Thank you for telling me. Was there anything else?"

"Don't know how significant it is, but I kept hearing piano music in the background."

Caroline just nodded her head. "Anything else?"

"No, nothing else."

Caroline looked at her watch. "Oh, look at the time, I should be going. Is there any way I can contact you?"

The gypsy appeared to be thinking. She fished around in her oversized colorful cloth shoulder bag and retrieved a notepad. Quickly, she scribbled a number on it and handed it to Caroline. "This is my cell number." Then she was gone

Caroline examined the number, written in second grade penmanship. Her heart was thumping so loudly she thought everyone could hear it. Feeling a bit dizzy, she clung to the shopping cart until it passed. A child began to wail in the next aisle. The sound was like a slap in the face, jerking her back to stability. She hurried to the check stand and sped back to Luke's apartment with her purchases. After her encounter with the gypsy and her ominous message, Caroline felt weak and drowsy. She put the groceries away, but by the time she'd finished, she could hardly keep her eyes open. Shuffling into the guest bedroom, she lay down on the bed. *I'll just take a little nap before I pick Luke up.*

Caroline, why do you keep up this foolishness? You know you can't win—you never did when we were married, and you won't now.

"NO! NO! NO!" Caroline shouted into a thick fog of nothingness. Her words bounced hollowly back to her. "Grant, just leave me alone, please." Caroline jerked upright. Tears wet her cheeks, and she was more frightened than ever before. She looked at her watch, it was three thirty. *Luke!* She went to the bathroom and splashed cool water on her face, ran a brush through her hair, and reapplied her lipstick.

Now she was in a quandary—should she or should she not tell Luke about Grant and about running into the gypsy? After the night before, she knew what his reaction would be. *I wonder if the gypsy told me everything.*

"RIGHT ON time," Luke said, as he slid onto the passenger seat of his car. "How was your day?"

Caroline exited the vehicle and walked around to the passenger side. "You drive, Luke."

"Why? I thought you knew that I'm fearless. I taught my younger sister, Rosalie, to drive, and nothing can be more traumatic than that."

Caroline went around to the passenger side, opened the car door and jerked Luke out. "You drive!"

Luke gave her a puzzled look and elevated his eyebrows. "Something happened, didn't it?" he said.

Caroline adjusted her sunglasses and slid onto the passenger seat. "Yes. I'll tell you about it when we get to your place."

Still staring at her, Luke said, "Looks like we could both use a drink. I know a quiet little lounge that serves the best Hurricanes in the French Quarter. Okay?"

"'Kay," Caroline managed to whisper, biting back her tears.

Luke put the car in gear and gave Caroline's shoulder a squeeze before backing out into the street. She glanced at his profile. *Since he was right about the effect the cards would have on me, how am I going to tell him about my encounter with the gypsy?*

The lounge was furnished with worn wooden booths and the floor was covered in peanut shells. It was early, so there were few people sipping drinks. Soft music wafted through the slightly alcohol-tinted air, as Luke and Caroline selected a secluded booth at the rear of the bar. After their drinks were served, Luke reached across the table and took Caroline's hand.

"Come on, now. How can I help you, if you don't confide in me? But, first, let me apologize for the way I reacted about the tarot reading. That was childish and foolish and I'm ashamed of myself. I was fearful that the reading would depress you, even more. That's why I reacted like I did. Can you forgive me for upsetting you? I never want to hurt you, in any way."

"There's nothing to forgive. You were right from the beginning. That's part of what I want to tell you. I ran into the gypsy at the grocery store, this afternoon."

"Oh!" Luke said. "What happened?"

"Grant was talking to the gypsy during the reading. Her exact words were 'His message was simple. He kept saying you won't win, give it up. You have no choice.' She also told me she heard piano music playing in the background, as he spoke to her."

"That is unnerving. No wonder you're upset."

"That's not all. After I went back to your apartment and put the groceries up, I became extremely tired, so I lay down and instantly went to sleep."

"And, Grant made a visit?"

"Yes. Same message, 'Give it up, you won't win, never did and never will.'" Caroline kept her eyes down, as she stirred her drink. "I feel like I'm in a cul-de-sac. I just circle around and return to the same spot."

Caroline noticed the helpless look on Luke's face and immediately regretted telling him what had transpired. She didn't want to upset him or make him feel guilty.

After a few minutes, Luke finally suggested they go home. Caroline downed the last of her drink and nodded.

CHAPTER

10

As they sat together on the couch, each lost in their own thoughts, Caroline's cell phone rang. "That must be Paul, checking up on me," Caroline rose and retrieved her cell phone from the kitchen counter.

"Hello."

"Caroline, it's Paul. I've been trying to reach you all afternoon. The Senator is in the hospital, He had a heart attack and is in serious condition."

"Oh, no! When did that happen?"

"This morning. He was taken to the emergency room at St. Lawrence, in Charleston. The hospital tried to reach you, and when they couldn't, they called me. The Senator had both of us as contacts in his wallet. I was fortunate enough to get the morning plane out. Is it possible for you to come home, now, and be with your father?"

"Of course. I'll leave immediately," she said, looking at Luke.

"That would be good. I've been with him constantly, and he's been asking for you."

Caroline was instantly awash with guilt. "I'll make arrangements, as soon as we hang up. Keep me posted, if his condition changes."

"I certainly will. How soon can you be here?" Then after a slight hesitation, Paul added, "I should give The Senator an update to keep him from stressing. I thought you kept your cell phone with you."

"Yes, I do. I don't know why I didn't receive the calls. I will try to get the next flight out, so I can be there early evening." She checked her cell phone for missing calls, but there were none registered. *I've had my cell phone with me all the time. Could Grant possibly have the power to control even that?*

"Early evening? I thought you were in the Keys."

"Ah, yes, I was," Caroline felt trapped. "But... but we came to New Orleans, yesterday. Marcella, my friend, wanted to come up for the weekend, so we spent a few days, here."

"Oh, I see. Well, at least you're closer. I hope you can catch the evening flight. With such a short window, it may not be possible."

"All I can do is try. If I can't get a flight, I'll drive. That would take at least eleven hours, though, if I drove all night. I need to get ready, Paul. I'll let you know when I get to Charleston."

"Be sure you do. We'll be looking for you."

AS SOON as Caroline ended the call, Luke asked, "What happened?"

"The Senator, my father, had a heart attack. He is in grave condition. I need to get to him as soon as possible. May I use your computer to make a reservation?"

"Yes, of course, but make it for two."

"You're coming with me?"

"You bet. I wouldn't let you do this alone."

"I won't be alone, Paul is there."

Luke raised his eyebrows.

"Okay, point well taken. I'll make the reservation for both of us."

"I'll call my answering service and have my appointments for the next week changed. Here," Luke said, as he pulled his credit card from his wallet, "put them on this card."

"Oh, thank you. I don't have my card with me. I'll reimburse you."

"Don't even think about that, now. I believe the commuter, Cloud Nine, leaves in the early evening."

"I'm on it. You go get ready. My bags are still packed, so it won't take me long."

Luke went into his bedroom and was back in less than ten minutes. "I'm ready," he announced, holding up a duffel bag. When Caroline tilted her head, Luke added, "I always travel light."

"So it seems," Caroline said, looking at her two large pieces of luggage. She printed their confirmation. "The flight leaves in less than two hours, so we must hurry," she said, before noticing Luke had already left the room. When she finally located him, he was standing in the open doorway with both of their bags, waiting for her.

"That was fast!" she said, grabbing her jacket from the hall closet. "Here's your credit card. The tickets were under five hundred, roundtrip for both. Now, that's a bargain, considering the short notice. I left the return open-ended."

THE TRIP to Louis Armstrong International Airport was in-and-of-itself an adventure. Luke's driving bordered on reckless in order to get them there in time to catch their flight. Caroline sat, white-knuckled, as Luke's vehicle weaved in and out of traffic. When they finally arrived, Luke stopped and let Caroline out at the Cloud Nine entrance.

Looking up at the arrival/departure screen, Caroline exclaimed, "Luke, our flight leaves from Gate Twelve in less than fifty minutes."

"Gottcha. You go check us in," he said, as he helped a red cap transfer their luggage from the back of the Range Rover onto a dolly. "I'll get there in time to board. Hurry now!" Luke called to her. Then he steered the Range Rover back into traffic and disappeared into a parking garage.

Caroline shifted from foot to foot, as she endured the check in process. She tried calling Luke's cell. No answer. Once cleared, she proceeded to Gate Twelve. She sat in the waiting area, anxiously scouring the faces of fellow travelers, searching for Luke. When their flight was announced, she stalled, hoping Luke would appear, but no luck. She called him, again. Finally, she had no choice but to board the plane. When she handed the attendant her boarding pass, she said, "I'm expecting a gentleman to join me. His name is Quinton Lucas. He went to park the car and isn't here, yet. Is there any way we could wait a few minutes for him?"

"No, ma'am, if he isn't here by the time we close the gate, he'll have to take the next flight. You should go ahead and board, or you'll miss this flight, too."

Caroline took another quick look around but didn't see Luke. "Would you hold his boarding pass in case he shows up before the gate closes?"

"No, ma'am. That's against regulations. I'm sorry."

Caroline stuffed the pass back into her shoulder bag and looked over her shoulder one more time. "Thank you, anyway." She reluctantly joined the line waiting to board the plane. *Luke, where are you?*

Luke had been delayed in the parking garage. When he was finally able to park, he raced through the terminal heading for Gate Twelve. He made it just before the gate closed. As Luke snaked his way down the aisle, Caroline looked up.

"There you are!" Caroline squealed, unable to stifle her joy.

"Yep, here I am. It's been quite an adventure, thus far. Some poor bastard had his vehicle with a dead battery blocking the way to the second level."

"I tried to call you."

"I know, but I was so busy maneuvering in the parking garage I couldn't answer. Then when I finally parked, I had to run like hell to get here on time."

THE REST of the short flight was uneventful. They landed in Charleston on schedule at 5:47 p.m.

"We'll take a taxi to The Senator's mansion. I'm sure his car is there and, if we can find the keys, we can use it while we're here. Don't know about you, but I would like to freshen up a bit before heading for the hospital."

"I agree," Luke said, as he escorted Caroline to the first cab in line. The driver opened the trunk and got out to help Luke with the luggage. Luke waved him off. "I got it," he said.

"Thanks, buddy." Once Luke was settled in the cab, the cabbie asked, "Where to?" as he engaged the meter on the dash.

"2485 Autumn Ash Park," Caroline offered.

The driver whistled. "High rent district," he muttered, as he scanned the oncoming traffic, and then pulled out into the stream.

"Hmm, high rent district," Luke whispered impishly to Caroline. She slugged his shoulder. They settled back and enjoyed the ride.

"If nothing else, The Senator is a showman. He likes to impress people with his wealth and power. It's always been that way. My mother was a trophy wife, but I think he truly loved her. Oh, Luke. I pray he will be okay. It's way too early for him to go."

"I know how you're feeling," Luke said, squeezing Caroline's arm. "I lost both parents within a year of each other. I think Mother gave up after Dad died. He was her whole life, and she felt she had nothing left to live for. Rosalie and I had both left the nest and chiseled out lives for ourselves. I feel that, basically, Mother willed herself to die. The autopsy report was pretty vague. It just listed 'Failure to Thrive' as cause of death. Imagine that, failure to thrive, in today's world."

"Yes, that is pretty sad. How old were you when she passed?"

"Twenty one. She died unexpectedly of an aneurism which erupted in her aorta. I was away at college when it happened."

"I'm so sorry. It's hard to lose your parents, at any age. Where does your sister, Rosalie, live?"

"Rose married an exchange student shortly after she graduated from LSU. He whisked her off to *Gay Paree*."

"Paris! That is really leaving the nest. Have you ever visited her in Paris?"

"Not yet—it's on my bucket list."

"You goof! You're too young to have a bucket list."

"Never too young to plan ahead."

Caroline sat, thoughtful for a few moments "Have you ever tried to contact them?"

"Them? I talk to Rose a couple of times a month."

"Oh, I meant your parents."

Luke scrunched up his mouth, as he thought about it. Finally he said, "You're the only one I'd admit this to but, yes, in fact, they were the first ones I did make contact with. It was an uplifting experience, and I learned they were together and happy. After the feeling I got upon learning that, I became more determined than ever to help others find the same peace that I felt at that exact moment. I've learned a lot about feelings and dealing with them during my career. Especially mine. At the time Mom died, I wasn't sure I believed in the afterlife.

"It was when I actually was able to talk with my folks, that I did a complete turnaround and knew, yes, absolutely knew. there is an afterlife. I was filled with so much joy that I bubbled over. I was given that second chance to say the things we often leave unsaid and then find it's too late and live with regrets. Dad and I were always at odds. We just didn't see eye-to-eye. When I connected with him, the first thing I did was tell him how much I loved and respected him. I was moved to tears, when he told me he always loved me and just wanted me to be the man he knew I could be. That's why he was so hard on me. He also told me how proud he was of the man I'd grown into…" Luke stopped.

"Go on, Luke. I want to hear," Caroline said. She looked over and saw Luke dabbing at his eyes. She took his hand and kissed it.

After a few moments, Caroline said, "It surely must be gratifying to help people find peace in their lives. Do all of the readings come out, well, happy?"

Luke was again in control. "No, I'm sorry to say. I must confess I'm a fraud of some stripe. When the reading looks like it's going to go badly, I disengage and tell the client that I couldn't understand what was coming through, or that I lost contact. What good would it do to have some-one fret over a bad message?"

"I agree. There's enough bad news in a lifetime without adding more bad news from the afterlife. You're a good man, Luke. Thoughtful, sensitive, and considerate. I very much like those qualities about you."

Luke blushed and smiled in appreciation.

"Oh, look! There's our home," Caroline said, pointing up a steep hill in a very ritzy neighborhood.

"High rent district doesn't do it justice," Luke mused.

Caroline watched him ogle the grand old south-ern mansion, adorned with white columns support-ing the top two stories. The landscaping was plush and green and very well maintained. The grounds looked like a park. Large oak trees draped with Spanish moss lined the driveway, and an abundance of flowers, strategically placed, graced the setting.

Having circled the driveway of the mansion, the cabbie stopped at the front steps. He got out and took the luggage from the trunk. Luke had the fare ready, having seen the amount on the meter. He handed the man a ten dollar bill for a tip. "I'll take those." He picked up the bags.

"Thank you, sir. Have a great day." The driver climbed back into his cab and zoomed down the driveway.

"Are you sure this isn't a hotel?" Luke teased, as they walked up the front steps to the massive double doors.

"For all the love I experienced here, it may as well have been."

Holding the luggage and looking up at the three story structure, Luke muttered, "I suppose the bedrooms are on the third floor."

"How insightful," Caroline said, as she inserted her key into the lock. The door swung open. They stood, gazing inside.

Finally, Luke asked, "Where's the elevator?"

"You're standing on it." Caroline pointed to Luke's feet.

"Very funny. Don't you have a butler or houseboy?"

"We did. I don't know what happened to them."

"I do. They ran away."

Caroline playfully punched his arm. "Come on, ya big baby. I'll help you," she said, and took his duffel from his grasp. "Follow me!" she ordered.

"You're too kind," Luke said, as he struggled with Caroline's two large suitcases. Both were out of breath by the time they reached the landing on the third floor. The stairway reminded Luke of Tara's plush red carpeted circular staircase. In fact, the entire mansion could have been straight out of *Gone With The Wind*.

"Where to from here?" Luke asked. Caroline pointed down a large corridor and beckoned him to follow. "This is my room," she said, as she opened the door. "Just put my luggage down, anywhere." Luke entered a beautifully appointed room that was ultra-feminine. It was decorated in white and pink and bespoke of a time when Caroline was much younger. Pictures of her school days were clustered on her walls. Luke examined them.

"It doesn't appear that you've missed much, even though you went to a private school, judging from these pictures of you and your friends. Who is that geek with his hand on your shoulder in this frame?"

"That's Charles. Charles Lester Wadsworth, the Third. And, he's not a geek. He was captain of the rowing team and very athletic… besides being handsome, rich and smart."

"Hmm, are those your priorities?"

"No, of course not. I'm just defending Charles."

"Um hum." Luke picked up a picture enclosed in a pearl encrusted ceramic frame. "I'm guessing this is your mother holding you. You look just like her... both beauties."

"Why, thank you. Yes, that is Mother. I was three, at the time." Caroline carefully took the picture from Luke and placed it back on her vanity.

Luke put his hands in his pockets.

"All this is window dressing. My childhood wasn't that splendid. Come on. I'll show you to your quarters."

Luke was given a suite midway down the corridor. Caroline opened the door and ushered him in. Luke stared. The large suite consisted of a sitting room, bedroom, and private bathroom. It was masculine in every respect.

"Well, I feel very important to have been given the presidential suite."

Caroline furrowed her brow and said, "We have several broom closets, if you think you'd be more comfortable."

"Oh, no, I'll force myself to endure this environment, just to please you."

"Okay, no more whining. Let's freshen up and head for the hospital."

"Right you are. Ten minutes?"

"Works for me. I'll look for the car keys in Dad's bedroom," Caroline said, as she closed the door to his suite behind her.

Ten minutes later, the couple met in the corridor, and Caroline jangled the keys for Luke to see. "Found them," she said grinning. "Looks like Dad still drives a Cadillac."

UPON ARRIVAL at St. Lawrence Hospital, Caroline approached the information desk.

"May I help you?" a pretty teen asked. She wore a volunteer's pink uniform and her nametag identified her as Joslyn. Her pleasant tone set Caroline at ease.

"Yes. My father, Winston Schumann, is a patient. He had a heart attack. I just arrived and am anxious to see him."

"Is this your husband?" Joslyn asked.

"Ah, no. He's, um, an old family friend."

"Mr. Schumann is only allowed one visitor at a time. Sir, you will have to wait, here," Joslyn said, pointing to the waiting area.

Luke looked at Caroline. "You'll be just fine. I'll be here waiting for you—take your time."

Caroline smiled, "I'm counting on that." *Yet, dreading the encounter.*

She watched Luke stroll toward a comfortable looking chair and select a sports magazine from the adjacent table. He looked back at her and winked. That little gesture gave her the courage to proceed, and she turned toward the bank of elevators to face the inevitable.

MOVEMENT THREE
CRESCENDO

CHAPTER

11

Caroline tentatively pushed the door open and entered The Senator's hospital room. She was not prepared for the vision before her. Her father was ghastly pale and appeared quite frail. Quite a contrast from the last time she saw him, barely six months ago, at which time he was robust and his face had a healthy glow. She tiptoed to his bedside and touched his hand. He stirred and opened his eyes.

"Caroline, finally, you're here," he said.

"Yes, Dad, I came as soon as Paul called."

"HUMPH! Seems like I've been waiting an eternity for you. What day is it?"

"It's Thursday, Dad."

"THURSDAY? How long have I been here?"

"Paul called me this afternoon. You were admitted this morning."

"That can't be right, can it?" Caroline noticed the perplexed look on his face.

"Would you pour me a sip of water?" With a shaky finger, her father pointed to the pitcher on the bedside table.

"Of course." Caroline poured some water into a plastic glass with a sipping straw and held it to her father's lips.

"Thank you. I'm parched." He eyed her with large, liquid steel blue eyes. He may be frail, but a look, any look, from her father still caused Caroline's heart to skip a beat. A smile flitted into view, and he commented, "You look well. The Keys must agree with you."

"What? Oh, yes, the Keys."

"Paul is a bit worried about you, Caroline. He said you were different."

"Well, Dad, considering what I've been through, you think that's surprising?"

"Of course not. That's exactly what I told Paul. But, are you sure you're all right?"

"Yes, Dad. I'm just fine. It felt funny at first, coming home and not finding Grant there. I've adjusted pretty well, though, and eventually I'll accept the new situation for what it is. That all takes time."

"Of course it does. Paul fusses like an old woman." Her father seemed to struggle with a thought, and then he blurted, "He also told me you played a piece at the symphony that was very professional." Looking intently at his daughter, he said, "When did you learn to play the piano like a pro?"

Caroline looked around the room, searching for a plausible answer. She finally said, "You know, Dad, I lived with Grant for three years. He practiced all the time, night and day. I'd had to have been dead not to have picked up a few skills at the keyboard. Grant tried to teach me to play, but I was always mediocre—at least compared to him."

"HUMPH! Paul tells a different story."

Good old Paul. He always knew what side his toast was buttered on. Before Caroline could answer, a nurse entered the room and smiled at her patient.

"Well, now, how are we doing this evening?" she chirped.

"Not worth a damn, if you must know. When do I get outta here?" he barked.

"Now, now. You just got here. Don't you like us?"

"NO! I wanna go home." Pointing to Caroline, he said, "My daughter is here, and she will take care of me." Caroline blanched.

"Oh yes. He has been asking about you, almost constantly. It's a pleasure to meet you. My name is Rachel and I have the night shift in this wing. Despite his protests, I'm afraid your father will not be released for a few days—not even in your care. His condition was and still is very serious. He needs to be monitored by professionals."

"Oh, quite," Caroline replied trying to filter the relief from her voice. She absolutely did not want to be a nursemaid to her father. Being his daughter was trying enough. "I totally agree with you. My degree is in law, not medicine. I faint at the sight of blood."

Rachel smiled at Caroline's intended joke but didn't respond. She was busy journaling on a chart she had retrieved from the foot of The Senator's bed.

"WHAT! What do you mean 'a few days?' Why I have things that need to be attended to. I cannot stay here a few days!"

"Now, calm down, Senator. Getting excited is not going to help your condition. Here take these." Rachel put two small pills in the man's hand and watched him swallow. She then placed the chart back on the foot of the bed and gently patted his foot. "You're lucky to be alive. So, just take it easy. Whatever it is you need to attend to will be there when you're able. If not, I don't think universes will collide in the interim."

"HUMPH! What do you know?"

Rachel turned, winked at Caroline and exited the room.

"Damn hospitals. I'm on the board, here. You'd think I'd get better treatment. Damn heart attack, damn doctors. Damn everything."

"Dad, slow down. Don't get yourself so excited. You need to concentrate on recovering. That is your primary concern, or, at least, it should be."

"Oh, sure. Just sit by and watch my life go down the toilet. Is that what you're suggesting?"

"How are two or three days going to affect the rest of your life, in such a drastic way? If you don't comply, *this* may be the rest of your life. If they won't tell you, I will. You're in critical condition. You suffered substantial damage to your heart, and it's going to take some time to mend. Quit being so stubborn—some things cannot be bought—like your health, for instance."

Caroline noticed her father's eyes starting to close. She watched him shake his head as if trying to stay awake.

"What did that bitch just give me? I'm very sleep..." He then drifted off into a sound sleep. Loud snoring quickly filled the room.

Caroline gently tucked the sheet around his shoulders and left. When she reentered the waiting room, Luke stood.

"How is he?"

"Cranky, mean, and ugly, otherwise not doing too badly, considering the circumstances. As you can well imagine, he's a difficult patient and expects special treatment. He still hasn't grasped the fact that he is in critical condition." She was rummaging around in her purse for her keys when she suddenly remembered Paul. She slapped her forehead. "Oh, my God. I forgot to call Paul!" She pulled her cell phone out and frantically punched in numbers.

"Excuse me, you'll have to go outside to use that," Joslyn said. "I'm sorry, hospital rules."

Caroline smiled at her and hurried toward the exit. Luke was right behind her. She continued dialing Paul's number, as she scurried.

"Yes?" Paul answered.

"Paul, it's Caroline. I'm just leaving the hospital."

"Oh, I wondered what happened to you. I've been waiting for your call."

"I know and I'm sorry. I was so anxious to see Dad that I came straight to the hospital."

"I see." His tone gave Caroline the idea he didn't "see" at all. "How's he doing?"

"You know Dad. If they don't euthanize him, I'll be surprised."

"CAROLINE!"

"Sorry, Paul. Bad joke."

"Indeed! That was somewhat disrespectful, but I know you are only venting." A little calmer, Paul asked, "What are you doing for dinner?"

"Actually, Luke came with me, and we thought we'd have a quick bite somewhere and get to bed, early." Caroline looked at Luke, who was vigorously nodding his head in agreement.

"Oh, I see." Another slight pause, "How is it Luke is with you? I thought you were with what's her name, Marcella?"

Caroline felt trapped, again, and didn't offer an explanation.

Paul didn't push, but sounded irritated. "Well, then I'll probably see you tomorrow at the hospital. I plan to be there early, as I have to leave for home on the evening flight."

"Oh, for sure. Thanks for taking such good care of Dad, Paul. You always were a good friend, and we love you."

"And, I love the two of you, as well. You're like family to me."

"And, you to us. Until tomorrow." Caroline closed her phone and looked at Luke. "Well, we dodged a bullet—at least for tonight."

Luke smiled and took her arm, urging her towards the parking lot.

"Where do you suggest we grab this quick bite?" he asked.

After a thoughtful moment, Caroline said, "With Dad resting, we have time on our hands. I'm taking you to *Greasy Fingers*. You're in for a treat."

"Have you ever noticed you have an interesting array of eating places in your history?"

"Yep, thanks to The Senator, I had a culinary education. *Greasy Fingers* has the best ribs this side of the Mississippi. If Dad weren't temporarily indisposed, that's where he would be taking us."

"I'm game. I'm also starved."

"Me, too. Get in. You still feeling brave? I'm driving, since I know my way around these parts."

"Too weak to fight. Besides, your driving could never compete with Rosalie's, in the scare department. She had, and still has, the market cornered."

AFTER DINNER, as they were driving home, Luke said, "You were right, those ribs were pure heaven. If I stay here long enough, I'll have to invest in a new wardrobe."

"That's the problem with southern fried hospitality—everything is not heart friendly. Probably contributed quite a bit to Dad's condition. With his stogies and his daily intake of bourbon, it's a wonder his heart is still pumping. Appears he is not out of the woods, yet, but if he complies with his restrictions, he'll make it. His nurse gave him a hefty dose of sleeping aids, and I'm prohibited from seeing him, again, until tomorrow. It's such a lovely night, how'd you like to go for a ride on a riverboat?"

"Riverboat? You're kidding. And, just where would we do that?"

"I thought you just might accept my invitation, and we're almost there, Charleston Harbor, that is. The riverboat, *Southern Belle,* has a ninety minute cruise which will take us past approximately sixty landmarks and points of interest. My favorite is the *Painted Ladies.* That's a row of antebellum mansions painted different pastel colors, lined up along the river front. Very impressive. You'll also be exposed to some of the history of the Holy City," Caroline said, as she expertly maneuvered the Cadillac into a parking space.

Luke leaned forward, staring out of the windshield, "Man! Just look at that baby! She's lit up like a Christmas tree," he remarked, "and, she's just sitting there, waiting to be boarded."

They exited the car, and Caroline ceremoniously took Luke's hand, pulling him along behind her like a mother leading her small child.

"Look," Caroline exclaimed. "The ticket line isn't long, at all! I remember Nettie would bring me down here a couple of times a month when I was home from school, and we'd have to stand in line twenty to thirty minutes to get tickets. It was worth the wait—I loved it—still do. And…you will love it, too."

Luke squeezed her hand. "I'm already loving it! I could get used to being pampered."

"Of course, you could!"

CAROLINE PURCHASED their tickets and, once aboard, the couple stood at the starboard rail. They watched the city slide by, as the cool summer breeze came off the Mississippi River. A pipe organ filled the night with southern favorites. Luke put his arm around Caroline's shoulders and pulled her close to him. They stood like that the entire cruise. When they arrived back at the mansion, Caroline parked the car in the oversized garage.

"Thank you! That was an unexpected pleasure," Luke said, pulling her close for a kiss on her lips.

Caroline had been waiting for that kiss all evening and responded wholeheartedly. After a while, she pulled back and lingered in Luke's embrace. She felt his breath gently brush the hair on the top of her head. In his arms, everything seemed at peace, and she savored this moment. Not far from her mind was her dad's health, Grant's shenanigans, and her own mental health. But at least for now, with good food and great memories and two very loving arms around her, the future had a chance to be happy.

She looked up and her gaze was met by Luke's. Embarrassed at being caught with blatant affection on her face, she pulled away and said, "I needed to reacquaint myself with Charleston. Couldn't think of a better way to do it than the boat ride. Actually, Luke, I love this city. It's so southern and so rich in history. If it wasn't for being so close to The Senator, I'd consider moving back."

Luke asked, "What's wrong with New Orleans?"

"What? Oh, nothing. I love the Big Easy, too," she replied. "Who wouldn't?"

Luke reached out and gently stroked her arm. "For your peace of mind, I had a revelation that your father's condition is stabilizing, and he will have a full recovery in time. He is resting peacefully, as we speak."

"It's not that I doubt you," Caroline replied, entering the kitchen and closing the garage door behind them. She picked up the phone, "I still want to call the hospital and at least leave a message. That way he'll know I really *do* care."

After a short wait, Caroline was transferred to her father's ward.

"Good evening, this is Rachel. How may I help you?"

"Rachel, this is Caroline, Senator Schumann's daughter. How is Dad doing?"

"Hello again, Ms. Schumann." Caroline didn't correct her when she used her maiden name. "The Senator is resting peacefully and has been all evening." Caroline smiled up at Luke, letting him know his revelation was accurate.

"Would you let him know I called when he awakens?"

"Yes, of course, I will."

"Thank you, Rachel. I'll be there early tomorrow morning."

Ending the call, Caroline turned to Luke, and asked, "Would you like something before we call it an evening? Hot chocolate, maybe?"

"Yes, I would. I've become addicted to our nightly ritual."

"Yes, me, too."

LATER THAT night, Luke was awakened by a violent rainstorm. On his way to the bathroom, he walked to the French doors that opened onto his third-floor veranda and peered out. The rain was coming down in buckets. After returning from the bathroom, he slipped into bed and, pulling the sheet up, he felt the presence of another body next to him.

"WHAT THE..." he cried, jumping up before he realized it was Caroline.

"The storm woke me, and I became anxious that Grant would make his usual rainstorm appearance. I just couldn't be alone. So, I slipped in—you were in the bathroom. I didn't mean to startle you."

Luke gathered her into his arms and held her in a tight embrace. "I hope that's not the only reason I find you in my bed."

Caroline snuggled her head into Luke's chest and kissed him on the underside of his chin. "There may be others." She giggled.

"I do believe that's the first time I've heard you giggle. It's sweet. Now, care to share those other reasons with me?"

"You're the medium, you tell me."

"Okay, this reading is free of charge. Hmm, I'm getting vibes that you find me irresistible and every moment we spend apart is pure torture for you."

"Wow! You are good. What else?"

"Oh, here's the best part, you're madly in love with me and want me to take you in my arms and take you places you've never been—and beyond."

"I do believe you've got it." Caroline stood and slipped the spaghetti straps of her nightgown from her shoulders. The gown fluttered to the floor. Moonlight had pierced the heavy rain clouds and danced across the room creating an illusion taking the lovers from reverie to realism in less than the blink of an eye. The two were soon lost in the throes of each other, oblivious to the extraneous. Neither the outside world nor the past would interfere this night with their first intimate encounter.

CHAPTER

12

The next morning, Caroline awakened early. Luxuriating in the perfume of last night's lovemaking, she was loathe to get out of the warm sanctuary of their bed and get dressed, but she did, anyway. While preparing breakfast, she took out every detail of their encounter and burrowed her face into it, breathing it into her heart and mind. *Could it be? Had she found love again, so soon after Grant's death? Was it too soon? What would people say? What would Dad say?* She shuddered at the thought, dissipating her reverie. Just then, a disheveled Luke appeared at her elbow and kissed her temple.

"Do you always get up before the chickens?" he asked, shuffling over to the coffee pot and pouring himself a mug.

"Usually. I've always been an early riser. When I attended Tulane, I would have my homework done before my roommate opened her eyes. But, then again, she could sleep through Sherman's assault on Atlanta. How do you want your eggs?"

"Caroline, I get the feeling you're avoiding our, you know…?" His ears began to turn red, and Caroline thought it was the most adorable thing she'd ever seen.

"Our what? Oh, you mean last night." She smiled shyly. "I don't regret a moment. That is, if you don't." Caroline suddenly felt unsure. Maybe Luke was sorry it happened. "We're both adults and knew what we were doing. Do—do you regret it?"

"Not in the least. In fact, I'm hoping it's the beginning of a new era in our relationship. And, I'm not referring to the professional one."

"So was I. But, Luke, I was raised southern, and proper southern women don't talk about sexual encounters—not even with other women. I'm not even able to discuss sex with my doctor." Caroline took a deep breath. "However, it was the most incredible night I've ever had. And that's all I'm going to say about it. For now."

"No problem. May I kiss you, again?"

Caroline put her whisk down and opened her arms.

A half hour later, Luke said, "I'll have my eggs sunny side up—to match my current mood."

THE SENATOR was sitting up in bed when Caroline entered his hospital room. Paul was sitting at his bedside. They seemed to be engaged in a serious conversation and quit speaking as soon as Caroline appeared.

"Well, Dad, you're looking better this morning. Good morning, Paul. Am I interrupting something?"

"No, no, not at all. We were just discussing some, ah, some financial business," Paul said. "I'll leave now, and let you two have some privacy."

"No need for that, Paul." Caroline sensed Paul was lying and wondered what they were secretly discussing. "You're as much a part of this family as anyone. I truly do not know what we would do without you."

"Why, thank you, Caroline.

"HUMPH!"

"Oh, Dad! I didn't mean to ignore you. How are you feeling, today?"

"Like going home, that's how I feel. I cannot tolerate another night in this place. It's cold, sterile, and lonely." Then he looked up and asked, "Paul, weren't you going to check with the doctor to see if I can be released? Since Caroline is here..."

"Yes. I'll go do that, right now," Paul turned his attention to Caroline. "But, don't leave before we have a chance to chat."

"Okay. I'm sure I'll be here when you get back."

As soon as Paul closed the door, Caroline's father motioned for her to sit in the chair Paul had just vacated. Caroline sat down, albeit tentative and apprehensive. She perched on the edge of the chair. She didn't know what the subject of the conversation would be but sensed she was in for an interrogation. That was a sport her father relished, beginning with her teen years.

"Caroline, Paul tells me you've been seeing someone, Luke something-or-other. How can you justify that? Grant is barely in the ground, and you're already gallivanting around with another man. Well, it just doesn't look right. What will people think?"

Caroline bristled. "Dad, first of all, I don't care what people think! Haven't you noticed, it doesn't matter what you do, someone will criticize you for it. Even the righteous have detractors."

"Don't you take that tone with me, little girl!"

"I'm not a little girl. And, since when do you have the right to discipline me? You were never around when I needed love and guidance, and now you're trying to be the all-caring father figure. It's not me you're concerned about, it's *your* precious reputation."

"How dare you speak to me like that!"

"How dare me? You're kidding! You were never in my life except when it suited you, and you don't know much about me. All I ever was to you was a nuisance. You may have planted the seed, but that was as far as your involvement in my life went. Even today, you're not concerned in the least how I feel or how I'm faring. You're only concerned about how I might be perceived by your so-called friends."

Caroline suddenly went wide-eyed, as she watched her father turn red, grab his chest, and wreath in pain.

"AAHHHH! Caroline, doctor, call the doctor, I'm..." he gasped, still grabbing at his chest. The alarms from the heart monitor had already activated and the noise was deafening.

"Oh, my God! I've killed him!" Caroline cried, as she tore out the door. "HELP, HELP, HELP, somebody, please help!"

The cardiac team was already in motion and, pushing the crash cart before them, they almost mowed Caroline down, getting into her father's room. Trying to get out of the way, Caroline pressed herself against the wall and watched the flurry of activity, as the medical personnel swung into action.

"You have to leave, now," a drill sergeant of a nurse ordered. "Go to the waiting room and someone will update you, as soon as we get him stabilized."

Caroline turned and raced toward the waiting room. When Luke saw her, he jumped up and caught her as she fell into his arms.

"Caroline, what happened?" Luke held her close.

"I think... I think... I think I killed him, Luke. I think I killed him," Caroline gasped between sobs.

"No, no, sweetie. You didn't. He's going to be all right, trust me on this. Why don't you tell me what happened?"

Before Caroline could speak, they heard Paul bellowing behind them.

"WHAT IN HELL'S NAME HAPPENED IN THERE?" Paul approached the couple.

"HEY! Take it easy, Paul," Luke said. "I'm trying to find out. Caroline is extremely upset. She can barely talk, so just sit down and cool your jets."

"You, young man, will show me some respect."

"I'll show you respect when you earn it. You can't just rush in here, acting like a crazed person, and demanding to know what happened. You could exercise some patience and compassion. Caroline will tell us in her own time." Luke put a protective arm around Caroline. "In the interim, she needs our support."

"Yes, well, I suppose you're right. But, The Senator was doing just fine when I left not twenty minutes ago."

Luke took Caroline's hands in both of his and calmly asked, "Can you tell us what happened?"

Caroline pulled her hands away and dabbed at her eyes with a tissue. She took a deep breath before she began, "We…we were talking about, " Caroline paused, *I can't let Luke know he was the catalyst,* "well, about my childhood and all of the sudden the alarms went off and, and, well, you know the rest." Caroline slumped into a chair and buried her head in her hands.

"Hmm," Paul scratched his head. "I don't understand, he was fine when I left. He asked me to negotiate his early release from the hospital, but

I guess there's no need for that, now," he muttered. Then he looked at Caroline, "He's counting on you staying and taking care of him when he's released, did you know that?"

"NO!" Caroline jumped up from her chair. "I can't. The Senator can hire a professional caregiver. I refuse to take on that kind of responsibility!"

"Now, is that any way to treat your father?" Paul chastised.

"Easy, Paul," Luke cautioned with a stern look.

Caroline sniffed and pulled herself upright. "Well, Paul, since you put it that way. He may be my biological father, but he has never been a real father to me. I'm not going to put my life on hold, waiting for him to—"

"That's enough, Caroline," Luke said. "This matter can wait until we know what the circumstances are."

As if saying it made it happen, a young doctor walked into the room, his face stern with news. He took his glasses off and slipped them into his shirt pocket. "I'm Dr. Logan. Are you Caroline Alexander?

"Yes. How is my father?"

"He has had a severe setback. We're moving him to critical care for a couple of days. Right now, we're in a wait-and-see transition. I'm advising he not have visitors for at least two days." The doctor furrowed his brow and asked, "Were you with him when he relapsed?"

"Yes," Caroline said, wringing her hands.

"Any idea what brought on the relapse?"

Caroline hesitated and then shook her head. She didn't see the need to fall on her sword. "We were talking about the past, and then suddenly he grabbed at his chest and the alarms went off."

"I see."

Just then, the hospital intercom interrupted their conversation, "Dr. Logan, you're needed in emergency. Dr. Logan, to emergency."

Dr. Logan said, "We have your contact information, and we will keep you posted."

"Thank you, doctor," Paul said, as he looked suspiciously at Caroline.

Caroline met his eyes and raised her chin. *He should shoulder some of the blame. After all, he was the one that told Dad about Luke.*

AFTER EXITING the hospital, while they stood in the parking lot, Paul said, "Caroline, your father told me he was going to talk to you about something. Did he bring up anything after I left?"

"Ah, yes, we talked about my childhood."

"Nothing else?"

Luke was paying close attention to the conversation.

"I don't know what you're referring to, Paul," Caroline said, plunging her hands deep into her jacket pockets.

"Oh, never mind. If he didn't say anything, then neither shall I." Paul shifted from foot-to-foot. Caroline noticed his impatience. *Holy God. I hope he doesn't say anything about Luke.* Finally, Paul pulled his car keys from his pants' pocket. "I'm afraid I must leave and get back to New Orleans. I have a practice that requires my attention. How long do you plan to stay here?"

"Depends on what happens. At least until Dad is out of the woods."

"Are you going to stay, Luke?" Paul asked, jingling his keys in his hand.

Luke drew closer to Caroline and said, "Why, yes. I don't want to leave Caroline alone during this critical period."

"I see." Paul swiveled to face Caroline. "Be sure to keep me posted on your father's condition, will you?"

"Of course, I will, Paul. You know I will."

Paul gave Caroline a perfunctory hug and the traditional goodbye kiss on the forehead. Looking as if he was giving it some thought, he held out his hand to Luke before bidding them goodbye. Luke and Caroline watched Paul drive away. When he was out of sight, Luke turned to Caroline and asked, "What was Paul referring to? I know you know, now tell me. Was it about me?"

"Yes."

"And?"

"Let's go home, and I'll tell you the entire story. I'm suddenly exhausted."

"Do you want me to drive?"

"Will you? My head is spinning and I'm feeling nauseous."

Luke opened the passenger door and helped Caroline inside. He even fastened her seatbelt. She looked pale and distracted.

"Maybe we should go back inside and have *you* checked out."

"NO! I'll be all right. It's just, it's just, oh, Luke, I caused his relapse. I was arguing with him. I'm so ashamed. I should have known better. Please, just take me home and I'll tell you everything that happened."

Both were silent on the drive to the mansion. Once inside, Luke hung their jackets in the coat closet off the foyer. "Are you hungry?" he asked.

"Oh, no. I'm too upset to eat, but you go right ahead. I think I'll lie down for a while."

"No you don't, not until you fill me in."

"Oh, Luke," Caroline whispered, "just hold me for a minute. I'm so upset and ashamed, I could die."

Taking her in his arms, Luke said, "I'm being insensitive. Of course, if you're not up to talking about it now, it can wait. Why don't you go lie down for a while? I'll be right here when you're feeling better."

"I intend to tell you, but, if Dad dies, it will be all my fault and I don't know if I could live with such guilt. What I did was stupid and childish."

"He's not going to die. I'll help you decipher the circumstances when you're up to it."

Caroline pulled her lips into a contrived smile. "Okay, but promise you won't hate me."

"I could never hate you."

Caroline flopped down on the sofa and patted the cushion beside her, motioning for Luke to take a seat. She then told Luke about her conversation with her father. When she finished she waited for the judgment to descend on her. Luke touched her cheek, instead. "Sweetie, he was in critical condition before you arrived, and that wasn't your doing. What you said only reminded him of his failings, and he just couldn't face it. My sense is he's been suppressing his feelings for quite some time. You told me his way of solving problems was to throw money at them rather than facing them head on and resolving them. That obviously didn't work in your case. You both need to forget the past with all the hurts and bad memories and get on with life."

"But, if I hadn't challenged him, he wouldn't have had the relapse. Don't you see, it was my fault?"

"Blessing in disguise. If he is that fragile, it's best his specialist knows before releasing him. My hunch is that between Paul and your dad, they would have coerced Dr. Logan into releasing him before he was ready. The next time, the cardiac team and crash cart may not be so accessible. So, my dear, you probably saved his life, not shortened it. I think you'll have more opportunities to make amends."

"You really think so?"

"Absolutely! Come on, let's go back to *Greasy Fingers*. I haven't gained the requisite five pounds yet, today."

"No way! You're going to eat salad and cold chicken. I don't want to be an enabler and responsible for your premature demise."

"Ouch! You're already killing me. I had my teeth set for—"

"A lovely green salad with light dressing—right?"

"Yeah, right. You're a hard woman."

"You ain't seen nutin' yet, cowboy."

"Why are you looking at me funny?"

"Oh, I was just realizing how you have a knack to bring me out of the doldrums."

SEVERAL DAYS later, Caroline received a telephone call from Dr. Logan saying The Senator's condition had stabilized, and he was on the mend. She was also told that he could be released, if and when someone was able to stay with him around the clock.

"I've engaged a medical service, TeamMed, to be here until you give the go-ahead that he can be on his own," Caroline told Dr. Logan.

"I know them and have a great deal of confidence in their ability to handle crises. In fact, they trained here at St. Lawrence, and I was involved in that training. I'm willing to release your father under those conditions."

"Thank you, doctor. How soon may we pick him up?"

"I'd prefer to send him home by ambulance. The ride will be smoother and easier on him, plus there will be a medical team on board. He will be released first thing tomorrow morning, assuming TeamMed will be meeting him upon his arrival."

"I have them on standby. I will telephone them as soon as we hang up."

"Good, and I will authorize your father's release with the instructions we discussed. Do not hesitate to call me should the need arise."

After Caroline hung up the phone, Luke said, "Honey, I have to get back to New Orleans and take care of business, or go on welfare. My clients have been patient, but I don't want to push the envelope. Since we engaged a medical service to have some-one here, day and night, your father should be all right. He'll probably be delighted to have round-the-clock attention."

"Don't you know it? Wonder how much more the team charges for verbal abuse. Whatever it is, they will more than earn their salaries. I know you have to get back, and I'm so grateful that you stayed this week with me. It was fun introducing you to Charleston. As soon as Dad is settled, I'm outta here. Will you meet me at the airport?"

"Hell, if I could fly, I'd come get you."

CAROLINE CALLED TeamMed and firmed up their engagement. She arranged to have a hospital bed delivered to The Senator's mansion by late afternoon. Luke helped Caroline transform her father's den into a hospital room, with all the amenities, but not interfering substantially with the ambiance cultivated over the years by her father.

"The least disruptive we can make Dad feel, the better," Caroline said, as the two stood back and admired their afternoon's handiwork. Glancing at the grandfather clock standing next to the doorway, Caroline added, "It's getting late. I've thawed some T-bones. If you'll grill them, I'll bake us a potato and toss a salad."

"Deal! How 'bout we celebrate homecoming with a glass of wine. I noticed your dad had a couple of bottles waiting to be claimed in the fridge."

"Of course, I should have thought of that. We'll be doing him a favor by consuming his alcohol, since he shouldn't have it, anyway. Remove the temptation, as it were." Then looking around, Caroline suggested, "We should search the place. He probably has bourbon and cigars hidden in every nook and cranny."

AFTER DINNER and cleanup, Luke took Caroline's hand and led her up the two flights of Tara stairs, as he liked to refer to them. "This must have been your training course when you were growing up," Luke said, wheezing. "It's quite a workout just getting to your room."

"You know, when you're a kid, you're tireless. The stairs never deterred me. I probably ran up and down them, ten times a day. I think Nettie grew tired of the constant up and down, in her later years."

"No doubt," Luke said. "This is even hard on a soon to be middle-aged man."

The two proceeded down the wide corridor after reaching the third floor landing. Caroline stopped at her bedroom door. Luke still had her hand and kept walking pulling her along beside him.

"Sorry, Lady. This bus doesn't stop here. You have to get off at the next stop."

"And, just where would that be?"

"I believe it's just this side of heaven."

And so it was.

THE NEXT day Luke brought his duffel bag down with him and set it in the foyer. After breakfast, he took Caroline in his arms. "I'm going to miss you like crazy."

"Probably not as much as I'm going to miss you."

"Let's hope your next few days are quiet, and Grant doesn't—"

Caroline placed a forefinger over Luke's lips. "Don't even say it! So far, so good."

The taxi that Luke had called honked from the driveway, heralding its arrival.

"There's my ride. You gonna be okay until I see you, again?" he asked, with concern in his eyes.

"Not really, but guess I can live with it. I'll be thinking about you every minute of every hour of every day," Caroline responded. "What about you?"

"Same here," Luke said. He rubbed at his eyes. "Damn allergies," he sniffed. "Don't know how I ever got along without you."

After one last, lingering kiss, Luke forced himself to pull away from Caroline's embrace. She stood on the veranda and watched until the cab was out of sight. It was now time to focus her attention on her father. Caroline vowed to forget the hurts of the past and foster a more loving relationship with him. There was a fine line between love and hate, and Caroline was determined not to cross the line.

THE SENATOR arrived the next day right on schedule and was ushered into the make-shift hospital room by the ambulance crew.

"I wish you'd reconsider and stay. I don't like the idea of strangers running the house or me, for that matter," Caroline's father said gruffly, as she tucked the sheet around his shoulders.

"You'll be just fine, Dad. I did the homework and am confident you're in good hands. In fact, this team can do a much better job than I. They are medically equipped for any emergency and they also know how to prepare heart-healthy, tasty meals."

"HUMPH! Heart-healthy, *tasty* meals. That's an oxymoron. More like dog food."

"Yep, you're improving. It's good to see you returning to your normal obnoxious, cranky self. God help TeamMed. They're going to need all the heavenly assistance they can get."

"HUMPH! A lot you care."

Caroline ignored the jab and, as soon as her father was settled, she announced, "I'm going to go pack. Your caregivers will be here soon, but if you need anything before they arrive, just call me."

Picking up the television remote, her father asked, "What time is your flight?"

Caroline was already half way up the staircase when she answered, "Five, this evening. I'll be in New Orleans by seven. I'll call as soon as I can. I spoke to Paul this morning, and he said he would come see you this weekend."

"Well, at least *he's* a good friend."

Caroline was tempted to respond, but chose not to. She didn't want to chance causing her father another setback. As she was packing, she remembered leaving her cell phone plugged in on the kitchen counter. As forgetful as she had become over the last few months, she decided to retrieve it immediately. She hurried down the stairs and, as she was going past the den, she looked in on her father. Caroline was shocked when she saw him. He was ghastly pale, almost blue. She rushed to him. As she approached, she observed the oxygen tube had fallen from his nostrils and was lying in his lap. She snatched it up and reinserted it in his nose. Immediately, the oxygen began flowing back into his lungs. Caroline dabbed at the perspiration on his brow with a tissue and in an anxious voice called to him, "Come on, Dad! Wake up, please, Dad, wake up!" After a few moments The Senator began to stir and color gradually returned to his face.

"Dad! Dad! Can you hear me?"

"What? What happened? I must have dozed off."

"You were almost comatose. You've got to be more careful. You dislodged the oxygen tube from your nostrils."

"HUMPH! I did no such thing. I would've known if I had. You trying to kill me off?"

"That's not even funny." Then after a slight pause, Caroline said, "I have to finish packing."

Upon retrieving her cell phone, Caroline went back to her room and resumed her task. Just as she finished, she heard the medical team arrive. She hurried down the stairs to greet them. They were cheerful and full of promise. *Too bad, The Senator will take care of that, in short order.*

"Hello. You're right on time. I'm preparing to leave. I have to be at the airport in an hour."

"HUMPH! She's deserting me in my time of need," her father interjected.

Caroline rolled her eyes in mock disgust and made the introductions. She asked, "Would one of you assist me with my luggage? It's in my room, on the third floor."

The med called Jimmy, stepped forward, "I'll be glad to. Just show me where to go."

As Caroline led Jimmy up the stairs, she said, "I left my contact information by the phone in the kitchen. You should be aware that I just discovered my father has a tendency to pull the oxygen tube from his nose, so please watch him closely. If he, er, if things become too difficult, call me."

Jimmy rubbed the back of his neck. "We'll keep a close eye on him. Maybe he accidentally jerks it out in his sleep. That happens from time-to-time. I'll mention to him how important it is to be careful with the tubes."

"Thank you." Caroline looked around, making sure she hadn't forgotten anything. Satisfied, she held the door open for the laden Jimmy. "I just can't wait to get home."

When the luggage had been deposited in the foyer, Caroline went to be with her father while she waited for the taxi to arrive. "Dad, you behave and take care of yourself. Be careful not to pull the oxygen loose, again. I'll try to make it back, soon. Your care-givers know where to reach me, if I'm needed."

"HUMPH. If you cared, you wouldn't leave in the first place. And, I didn't touch the oxygen. I know I need it to survive. Are you sure you didn't accidentally dislodge it?"

Caroline threw her hands up in the air, her exacerbation almost tangible. Before she could respond, the taxi honked from the driveway. She jumped up, "Well, it's time to go." *Thank you, God. You saved me from killing him, at least this trip.* She planted a kiss on her father's forehead and headed for the door, calling out, "Dad, behave and follow your doctor's orders. I'll phone you as soon as I get home."

"Did you forget to tell me something?"

"You know I love you," she said, rushing out without waiting to receive a response. Once in the taxi, Caroline breathed a sigh of relief. *Free at last.* Something niggled at her, though. *I wonder how the oxygen came loose, if he didn't do it—and he's adamant he didn't. Surely, not Grant.*

LUKE SWEPT Caroline up in his arms and swung her around, as he greeted her upon her arrival at the airport.

"Luke, we've only been separated a few days," she gasped. He was holding her so tightly she could barely breathe.

"Seems like a lifetime," he joyously said. "How's your father doing?"

"I think he's much better than he'll admit. His color is good and he's cranky as hell—signs that life is returning to normal."

"Come on, let's get your luggage and get out of here." Then Luke added, "I take it nothing happened, or you would have said something."

"You mean Grant? I'm not sure." Caroline told Luke about the oxygen incident.

"Let's not jump to conclusions. It seems more likely that your father inadvertently disconnected, as he slept."

"He swears he didn't, and I'm inclined to believe him. Would Grant be able to do that?"

"I don't know."

"I wish I had some answers."

"I wish I had some for you." Luke pulled Caroline close, as they waited at the Cloud Nine carousel for her luggage.

CHAPTER
13

Walking to the car after dinner, Luke asked, "Do you want to go to your house? You're certainly welcome to come home with me, if you're not ready to go home, yet."

"I think I'd like to go home, Luke. I haven't been home in a month."

"As far as I'm concerned, you *have* been home."

Caroline hugged his arm, "I know, but I get my mail at a different address. I've probably got a mountain of bills waiting for me. Tonight, I'm much too exhausted, both physically and emotionally to even think about it."

"Home it is, then. Oh, by the way, I called Amanda and told her you were out of town and wouldn't be able to keep your Thursday appointment."

"Oh, my gosh. I had completely forgotten about it. Thanks for doing that."

"No problem. Amanda was gracious and said she was looking forward to seeing you on Tuesday."

When they arrived at Caroline's abode, Luke transferred her luggage from his vehicle to the foyer.

"Want me to take these up for you?"

"I can manage, I think. Anyway, they can wait until tomorrow. I'm headed for the shower and then the sack."

"Let me take a look around before I leave."

"Good idea. And, since you're going up anyway, ah, you could take the luggage."

Luke smiled, "No problem, Scarlett."

Caroline pretended to bristle. "I'm too tired to tangle, mister, but I'll get even with you for that remark."

"I don't doubt that, in the least."

After a thorough walk-through, Luke was satisfied everything appeared to be in order. "Call me tomorrow, okay?"

"Okay, but not too early. I think I could sleep for a week."

"Easy on the pills," Luke said, giving Caroline a stern look.

"I know, I know. I'll be conservative."

Kissing Caroline lightly on the lips, Luke descended the stairway and left the residence.

AFTER CLOSING the front door, Luke tested it to make sure it was locked. Satisfied Caroline was safe, he jogged down the driveway to his car. Just as he was opening the driver's door, a bolt of lightning flashed in the south and drops of rain began to fall, refreshing the night air. Luke had always loved rainstorms, but with Grant's propensity to manifest himself in the midst of a storm, Luke became wary.

Before he climbed into his vehicle, he turned around for one last look. Noticing a light on in the upper level, Luke shook his head and hurried back to the door and rang the bell. A few seconds later, the outside light came on, and he saw Caroline peer at him through the etched glass windowed door.

She swung it open and, with a surprised look on her face, said, "Luke! I thought you were gone. It's raining!"

"That's why I'm not gone. Do you want me to stay the night, or do you want to come home with me?"

"You may as well come in before you get any more drenched. I don't have the energy to leave, even if I wanted to. Thank you for coming back. I was dreading being alone with another storm raging."

"I was dreading leaving you alone," Luke responded, as he shed his dampened jacket and hung it in the hall closet. At the top of the stairs, Luke asked, "By chance, you wouldn't happen to have a spare T-shirt in size XL would you?"

"No. But, I can give you two XS. You can put one on each arm."

"Never mind, I'll sleep in the buff." Noticing the expression on Caroline's face, Luke chuckled. "Don't look so shocked, I'm just kidding. I have a T-shirt on underneath this," he patted his chest, "and I seldom sleep without my boxers."

"You're taking advantage of my diminished state, but watch out! Tomorrow I'll be a formidable sparring partner."

"I'll hold you to that."

"Maybe you should just hold me," Caroline whispered.

"That can be arranged."

After the two embraced, Caroline gestured towards the end of the corridor. "You can use the guest bathroom. It's at the end of the hall. The bathroom cabinet contains everything you need: toothpaste, toothbrush, and washcloth. Don't forget to come back when you're finished."

When Luke reappeared, Caroline was already in bed. He crawled in beside her and pulled her into him, wrapping her in his arms. He gently kissed her. "Goodnight, honey, you're safe, now." Caroline quickly dozed off.

I wonder how many sleeping pills she has on board, was Luke's last thought before he, too, was sound asleep.

SHORTLY BEFORE midnight, Caroline jerked awake and woke Luke. "Did you hear that?" she whispered, her voice trembling.

"Sounds like the piano. You didn't leave the TV or radio on, did you?"

"No. Remember, we did a walk-through before you left. Nothing was on, then."

"Right."

"I'm afraid to think of what it is. It sounds all too familiar." Caroline pulled the coverlet up under her chin, as she spoke.

"I'm going to check it out," Luke said, as he moved to the edge of the bed.

"NO! Don't leave me here, alone," Caroline begged. She grabbed Luke's arm like it was a lifesaver.

"Then, come with me."

"No. Just don't go, please, Luke."

"I have to," Luke said, as he threw the coverlet back and swung his legs out of bed.

"Please!"

"Honey, we can't just lay here doing nothing. No harm will come to you. He's apparently downstairs," Luke said, gently prying her fingers from his arm. "I'll only be gone a few minutes."

Luke stealthily walked across the bedroom floor and opened the door. He peered out and then was gone.

ALMOST INSTANTLY, Caroline heard the clatter, as Luke fell full-force down the stairs. She jumped out of bed and ran to the landing. Luke was lying spread-eagle on the floor at the foot of the staircase.

"LUKE!" Caroline cried. She dashed downward, her bare feet slapping a staccato on the marble steps. She knew better than to try to move him for fear he may have broken bones. She did a cursory examination and determined he was breathing. Trying to calm her heartbeat, she grabbed the phone and dialed 911. She knelt by her lover, waiting for the dispatcher.

Luke stirred. "Caroline …"

Caroline dropped the phone and tenderly lifted Luke's head, cradling it in her lap. "Are you okay? Anything feel broken?"

Luke tried all his limbs, which moved without pain, but when he twisted his neck, he winced. "Nothing broken, but I think I sprained something. Here," he attempted to get up, "can you help me?"

Caroline took his arm and put it over her shoulder. She could hear the 911 dispatcher's voice asking what her emergency was, but she ignored it. "Let's get you to the stairs." They hobbled over, and Caroline slid Luke's arm off, as she eased him down. She ran back and got the phone. "False alarm," she said, before hanging up. With a big sigh, she settled next to Luke on the stair.

"I don't know what happened, but I don't think I fell."

"What! Are you sure?"

"Yep, dead sure. Well, *almost* dead, but not all that sure. When I felt myself falling I instinctively tucked my head and curled up in a somersault."

"Don't scare me like that, ever again. I don't think I could continue to live without you." Then Caroline bit her lower lip. "Do you think it was Grant?"

"I can't say, but I have my suspicions," Luke said, wincing from pain.

"Could he do that?"

"He can move car keys."

"Oh, my God. Now what do we do?"

Just then, they heard the cover of the piano keys slam down. They both jumped. Caroline edged closer to Luke. The roles were reversed, and it was now Luke who was attempting to calm Caroline.

"Luke, I'm scared to death. I can't let him hurt the people that mean so much to me. I'm going to do it. I'm going to give in, rather than see you or The Senator or Paul hurt or killed, because of my stubbornness."

"No, Caroline. If you give in to this, who knows what else he'll demand of you. I won't let you. Surrender is not the answer." Luke struggled to get up.

"Then, what is the answer? I've been living this nightmare for over four months, now, and I'm worn down trying to fight it. I don't feel like Amanda's suggestion will work—not now and not ever. Look at what just happened. Do you think my saying he can't control me will make a difference? He will find a way. He always has."

Caroline walked to the drawing room doorway and turned the light on. She glanced back at Luke, and saw he was holding the left side of his ribcage. He was standing, now, trying to walk. She knew he must be aching all over. She rushed to his side. "Let me help you."

Luke started to brush her hand away, but thought better of it. Instead, he leaned on her. "I'm going to get dressed and get your luggage. Good thing you've not unpacked, yet. You're coming home with me. Come on, I don't want to stay here, tonight."

"You know that's not the answer."

"No, but it's a band aid and will do until we can come up with something better."

Caroline put her arm around Luke's waist and helped him back up the stairs. "Good grief! I'm beginning to feel like a Nomad dragging my luggage from place-to-place for the last six weeks."

WHEN THEY arrived at Luke's apartment, Caroline found some aspirin in the medicine cabinet and gave Luke two tablets. Once they were settled in bed, Luke was soon sound asleep. Caroline lay very still listening to him gently snoring. *This is my problem, and I have to resolve the issue, one way or another. We're out of options. Dad and Luke*

practically getting killed were warnings from Grant. Tomorrow, I'm going to see Father Jonathan and ask him for an exorcism. Thus, having made a decision, she, too, fell fast asleep.

Caroline arose early and was already flipping potato pancakes when Luke appeared on the scene. "How are you doing? You look like you're in pain," Caroline said, as she helped him up on a padded stool at the counter.

"Just stiff and sore from the fall. I took some more aspirin and will be okay, as soon as I get to moving around."

Caroline nodded and pointed to the skillet on the range. "I'm making potato pancakes from an old family recipe. Hope you feel like eating something."

"Smells good, and yes, thank you, I am hungry." Luke pressed his hands against his ribcage and winced. He sipped coffee from the mug Caroline had set in front of him. Caroline served the pancakes and sat down across from him. She toyed with her breakfast, and finally said, "Luke, I'd like to use the car, today, if that's all right with you."

"Of course, as long as you don't go home."

"I promise, I won't.

"Okay, we need to leave, soon. I have my first appointment in twenty minutes."

"Are you sure you're up to it?"

"Have to be. Besides, I'll just sit behind my desk and not exasperate my injuries. It'll be all right."

As soon as they finished breakfast, Caroline cleared the dishes and grabbed her shoulder bag. Luke was waiting at the door. Arriving at his office, Luke groaned, as he leaned over and kissed Caroline before he departed the vehicle.

"Remember your promise. Don't make me hurt you."

"I remember," Caroline smiled and put the car in reverse. She headed in the direction of Holy Trinity Church.

"CAROLINE! BACK so soon?" Father Jonathan asked, as he walked up the aisle of the church to greet her.

"Father, I desperately need to talk to you."

"Should this conversation take place in the confessional?"

"No, nothing like that, but it is confidential. May we use your office?"

"Of course, my child. This sounds mysterious," the priest remarked, remembering the shock he received when he touched the cross a couple of weeks ago.

When they were settled in the priest's office, Father Jonathan asked, "Now, what's bothering you on such a lovely summer day?"

"Oh, Father, I don't know where to start."

"Well, the beginning would probably be the best place."

Caroline nodded and began to tell her story starting with the accident that killed Grant, the doctors giving her a transfusion, and Grant's appearances since the time she arrived home from the hospital. The priest listened intently and did not interrupt. She concluded by asking, "Father, will you perform an exorcism?"

The priest folded his arms and pursed his lips. After a long moment, he said, "I'm not sure that would solve your problem but, then again, what have we got to lose?"

"Thank you, Father," Caroline said. "I'm running out of options and am willing to try anything." She hesitated to ask her next question, but she needed to know. "Just exactly what happens during an exorcism?"

"Well, Caroline, exorcism is largely composed of prayers, appeals, and statements. I have a special stole and surplice that I wear. We pray for God to free the possessed from the bondage. I will command the unwanted spirit to leave your body and will sprinkle holy water and touch the possessed—that would be you—with a Catholic relic."

"Have you done this before?"

"A few times."

"Did it work?"

Father Jonathan fidgeted. "Hmm, unfortunately, my batting average is under 500."

Caroline furrowed her brow. "Fifty percent of the time is not all that encouraging. What kind of relic you do use in the ritual?"

"All Catholic altars have an object of a known saint embedded in them. We have what we believe to be a small bone of Saint Jude. I will press your forehead against the altar at the appropriate time."

"Saint Jude, he's the patron saint of lost causes. How appropriate." Caroline sat in silent contemplation for a few moments. "Let's do it. I don't want to wait another minute."

Father Jonathan nodded and rose from behind his desk. He approached a small wardrobe in his office and took out a purple stole and surplice. He donned the attire and then turned to Caroline. "We will pray together. It usually takes thirty to forty minutes to complete the process. Are you ready?"

"Absolutely," Caroline said, kneeling before the priest and bowing her head.

Father Jonathan prayed aloud and sprinkled holy water at various times. He put his hands on Caroline's head and raised his eyes skyward, asking God to release her from the bondage. He took her to the altar and pressed her forehead against the cool marble. He christened her with sacred oil. At the conclusion of the exorcism, the priest took Caroline's hands and helped her to her feet. "My legs are numb, Father," she said, as she sat down on the bottom step to the altar.

"That's a sign the Holy Spirit is working in you," he replied. Placing his hand on her shoulder, he asked, "How do you feel?"

"A little dizzy, but otherwise, not much different," Caroline said. Her voice was shaky.

"Now, don't be disappointed. Exorcism is not an instant fix. These things take time. Just like a physical wound, it takes time to heal."

"Time is not my friend," Caroline said, dejectedly. "I just hope all of this is not too little, too late." Picking up her shoulder bag and slinging it over her shoulder, Caroline rose and started down the aisle of the church.

Father Jonathan hastened to catch up to her, as she headed for the main doors of the church. Huffing a little, by the time he reached her, he said, "You sound cynical."

"Knee-jerk reaction, I guess. I'm just frazzled," Caroline replied, as she stood by the heavy paneled doors.

"Will you come back tomorrow—for a follow up," the priest suggested.

"Why, I could come back, tomorrow, I guess."

Raising his right hand and tracing the sign of the cross, Father Jonathan blessed Caroline, before she went out into the fresh morning air.

When it was nearing time for Luke to leave for the day, Caroline drove to his office and parked in his designated parking slot. While she waited for Luke, she pondered the folly of the exorcism and all the failed attempts to beat Grant at his game.

When Luke approached, he smiled, brightly. "Here I am. Have you been waiting long?"

"No, in fact, I just barely got here. How are you feeling?"

"Better. Perhaps the lack of movement helped relax the tenderness. Did you have a full day?" he asked, as he carefully arranged himself into his seat and buckled up. "What did you do?"

"I went to see Father Jonathan, and we did an exorcism."

"Oh, I see. And?"

"And, nothing. Nothing seems different. Just another exercise in futility, as they say." With pleading eyes, she said, "Luke, I'm just grasping at straws, now. I don't know which way to turn."

"I know you're frustrated, but don't give up hope," Luke said, squeezing her hand. "There is an answer to your dilemma. Even though I can't seem to help you, the divine can. Trust in the greater power. It will be in His time and way, and I don't mean Grant's."

"Hopefully sooner than later," Caroline said, as she bit her lower lip. "All I can envision now is failure."

THE NEXT day, Caroline retuned to the church.

"Caroline, you did come back. Are things any better?"

"No different. I can't tell if I'm free of my bondage. When will I know?"

"That's difficult to predict. Just be patient, my dear. We are in God's time, not ours."

"I've heard that before," Caroline mumbled under her breath.

"Pardon," Father Jonathan asked, raising an eyebrow.

"Oh, nothing." Caroline responded. "I had, ah, I had a friend, actually, one of my sorority sisters. She had a situation I'd like to ask you about."

"Certainly. What was it?"

"Well, long story short, her little brother needed an emergency kidney transplant, otherwise he would die. Her brother was put on a waiting list. His condition was critical. My friend felt her brother wouldn't live long enough to receive a kidney from the organ bank.

"The siblings had the same blood type, and she wanted to donate a kidney, but was told she wasn't strong enough to undergo the operation. Since she was twenty-one and could make the decision on her own, she insisted they at least try. Incidentally, this was eight or nine years ago, and to this day it still haunts me. My dilemma centers around her decision. Would submitting to certain death, in essence a suicidal act, constitute a mortal sin and eternal damnation?" Caroline folded her arms, waiting for an answer.

"That is certainly a moral dilemma, my child. However, I think the difference here is that she didn't *want to die*, but she loved her brother enough *to die* to save him. In the church's view, under the circumstances, that would not be considered suicide. You're familiar with John 15:13 which reads, 'Greater love hath no man than this, to lay down his life for his friends.'"

Caroline frowned and looked down at her folded hands. She finally said, "I see. So you're saying that if one person sacrifices his or her life to save another, it's not considered a sin or at least not a mortal sin?"

"It is no sin, at all!" Father Jonathan said, in an authoritative tone. "Caroline, what happened to your friend? Did she donate the organ and in the process die in the place of her brother?"

"Yes."

"And, how do you suppose her family, especially her parents and her little brother, felt? Her parents would have lost a child, either way. I would think her brother would also be guilt-ridden for the rest of his life, knowing that his sister forfeited her life for his. That doesn't sound like a positive ending, does it?"

"No, it doesn't."

"And, how is it the surgeon went ahead... "

Caroline didn't even try to contrive a response. She had an answer to her question—that was all she needed. Looking at her watch, she grabbed her shoulder bag from the floor beside her chair and exclaimed, "My! Look at the time, I must go. I, er, have an appointment. Thank you for your time, Father." She jumped up and rushed out without looking back.

FATHER JONATHAN frowned as he watched Caroline scurry from the church. He went back into his office and telephoned his cross-town counterpart, Father Murphy.

"Jonathan, what a surprise. Is it time for our weekly lunch, already?" Father Murphy said, in an Irish brogue.

"Patrick, I have a major problem I need your help with. It's critical! A matter of life or death."

"Okay, I'm listening, Jonathan. Hopefully, I can be of help."

"I believe a young women is about to take her own life. I need to summon help immediately but I don't know where she lives. Her name is Caroline Alexander."

"Hmm, afraid I don't recognize the name. Is she a member of my parish?"

"No, but she has a close friend who is. I've forgotten his name but he's a tall, good looking, muscular fellow. He goes by the first name of Luke. Does that sound like anyone you know?"

"Yes! I believe you're referring to Quinton Lucas."

"Yes, yes! That's it. How do I get in touch with him?"

"Hold on while I check the parish records."

Father Jonathan rubbed a hand through his thinning hair, as he waited for what seemed like an eternity. Finally Father Murphy came back on the line.

"Lucas is a physic and has an office in the French Quarter. Here is his phone number. 241-9032. What can I do to help?"

"Just stand by. If I can't get him I may ask you to run by his office."

"Why don't I do that, anyway, just in case? That would save time. What are the circumstances he should know about?"

"His friend, Caroline Alexander, met with me, today, and I fear she may be suicidal. That's all I have time to tell you, right now. Patrick, will you call me, as soon as you return to your office, and let me know what you learn? In the interim, I will try to reach Luke by telephone."

"I will. God be with you," Father Murphy replied, and hung up the phone.

"GOOD AFTERNOON. This is Quinton Lucas' answering service. How may I direct your call?"

"I have an emergency and need to speak to Mr. Lucas, right away."

"Please hold the line. I'll try to contact him. May I tell him whose calling?"

"This is Father Jonathan, and please hurry. This is a matter of life or death." The next voice Father Jonathan heard was Luke's.

"This is Quinton Lucas. How can I help you?"

"Luke, thank God I caught you. This is Father Jonathan. Caroline was here a few minutes ago, and I'm worried she might be suicidal... Hello?"

Luke dropped the phone and raced out of his office. Rushing from the building, he jerked open his car door and maneuvered his Range Rover out of the parking slot and, in a frenzy, raced to the highway. He was frantic. Exceeding the speed limit and making California stops, he tore through the French Quarter, headed for the city. His driving was so erratic, that he picked up a patrol car on the outskirts of the city. The officer gave chase with his siren blaring.

Good! That ought to clear the traffic out of my way. Luke continued to speed through the streets, only slowing for red lights so as to avoid becoming involved in an accident and hurting innocent people. The officer in the patrol car obviously called for backup because, soon, there were two more patrol cars in hot pursuit. Luke was surrounded by the three patrol cars, one on each side and one behind him. The policemen signaled for him to stop. Luke had no intention of stopping and increased his speed when traffic would allow.

The two patrol cars, one on each side of the Range Rover, finally relented and fell behind Luke. The parade streaked through the city streets and finally came to a stop in front of Caroline's mansion. As Luke jumped out of the Range Rover, he was greeted by three automatic pistols pointed his direction. The officers had taken shelter behind their vehicles.

"WAIT!" Luke shouted...

"HEY, you, Rambo, hit the dirt and put your hands behind your back," a stern voice ordered from behind the barricade.

"LISTEN TO ME, DAMN IT! There is a woman in that house who is about to take her own life if she hasn't already done so. I think we have time to save her, but we must hurry. Please, let me up."

Luke turned his head so he could see the uniformed officers. They were talking among themselves.

"WE'VE GOT TO HURRY!" Luke shouted, and started to get up.

"Take it easy, there partner," a tall, gangly uniformed officer ordered.

"Watch it, Rusty," Luke heard another officer say. "We don't know if he's armed."

"I'm not armed, I swear. I'm just worried that we may not reach my client in time."

"Okay, I'll take your word that you're not armed. But, I warn you, one false move, no matter how innocent, and you're Swiss cheese," the one called Rusty said, as he approached Luke from behind. "How do you know she's in there?"

"Father Jonathan told me. Please, I beg you. We're running out of time. You go inside. Just do something for God's sake."

"Father Jonathan from Holy Trinity?" Rusty asked, as he arched his eyebrows.

"YES!"

"Okay buddy, I'm going to let you up, but don't try anything fancy. We've already tried the front door. It's locked, and she doesn't answer the bell. We saw a car in the garage so I'm going to give you the benefit of the doubt. Tony, take Sal and go around back," Rusty said, jerking his thumb toward the west side of the mansion. "See if there is another entry to the house. You," Rusty said, pointing to Luke, "come with me."

Luke, Rusty, and the two other officers darted in opposite directions around the perimeter of Caroline's house, searching for an unlocked entrance. They came together at the back of the mansion on the patio.

"Nothing, Rusty," Sal said.

Luke looked at the glass French doors on the patio. *I'm going to do something even if it gets me shot.* He bent and picked up a brick from a flower bed and raised it in the air.

"HEY! Hold on there, Rambo. You can't do that. If you throw that brick it's breaking and entering, and you get a felony rap. If I throw it, it's a welfare check. Give me the damn thing." Luke handed the brick over and Rusty heaved it through one of the glass panes in the patio door nearest the lock. As soon as he did, Luke dashed forward and reached inside and unlocked the door. When the door was opened, Luke shouted, "UPSTAIRS!" and he and the uniforms raced to the staircase.

Luke slammed open Caroline's bedroom door hitting the inside wall with a loud bang. The door immediately bounced back, and Luke kicked it open, again. Caroline was curled up in a fetal position on her bed. Luke overheard one of the officers calling 911 requesting an ambulance. Rusty bent close and patted Caroline's face, trying to revive her, but she was non-responsive.

Luke hastened to the bathroom and retrieved an empty sleeping pill bottle. He rushed back to the bedroom and handed the bottle to Rusty. Sal had started CPR. Caroline was having trouble breathing and appeared to be in shock. Luke lifted her hand and felt her pulse. It was erratic. He feared she had already slipped into a coma.

The officers desperately worked over Caroline's limp body, trying to revive her.

"I've got her breathing," Sal said, as they heard the scream of an ambulance in the distance.

Luke could see from the window the ambulance, as it turned onto Caroline's street. Luke half ran, half stumbled down the stairs in his haste to get to the door to usher in the medical team. As soon as the paramedics were within ear shot, he shouted, "SHE TOOK AN OVERDOSE OF SLEEPING PILLS. She's on the second floor—follow me!" Luke led the medical personnel up the stairs, two at a time.

As soon as the paramedics entered Caroline's bedroom, the uniforms stepped aside to give them room to do their job.

"Do you know if the pills were prescription or over-the-counter?" one of the paramedics asked.

"Here's the bottle," Rusty said, and handed the empty bottle to the paramedic.

The paramedic looked at the bottle and raised his eyes to his partner. "The prescription was filled ten days ago and it was for thirty pills. If she took them as prescribed, two at a time, there were ten left in the bottle. We need to get her to the hospital, since there is no telling how many she actually took."

The paramedics carefully strapped Caroline to a gurney and, with the help of the officers, took her down the stairs and out the front door. Luke was close on their heels. As they loaded the gurney into the ambulance, Luke asked, "May I ride with her?"

"Against regulations," one paramedic said, as another waved him off.

Luke turned and ran to his Range Rover, but was stopped by Officer Rusty.

"I can't let you drive." Rusty pointed to the closest patrol car and said, "Hop into that car, and I'll take you. Give me your keys, and I'll have Tony follow, so you'll have your vehicle when you get ready to leave the hospital. I'm not going to give you a ticket. With all the traffic laws you broke, you'd be in the slammer for forty years, or more. Under the circumstances, I feel a verbal warning will suffice."

"Thanks for the break, Officer...and the ride. I'm still pretty shook up."

"I can see that. Get in, let's get going."

As the ambulance left Caroline's residence, Rusty's patrol car provided the escort with Luke's Rover and another patrol car close behind. The caravan of flashing lights careened through the streets of New Orleans and made its way to the hospital in what, to Luke, seemed like an eternity, but in reality was record time. Rusty stopped his patrol car behind the ambulance and, as soon as Caroline was unloaded, he turned to Luke. "Go on. I have to call in, and then I'm right behind you."

Luke jumped out of the patrol car and frantically rushed into the hospital, just as the emergency team was wheeling Caroline into an examination room. Since he was not allowed in the room with Caroline, he took up a position in the waiting area, as close to the examination room as possible. He paced up and down, wringing his hands and constantly peered down the corridor towards the emergency unit, praying for Caroline's recovery and daring not to think about what would happen in the event she didn't.

"LUKE." FATHER Jonathan approached the waiting room.

Luke jumped.

"Didn't mean to startle you," Father Jonathan said. "I've been praying for her. How is she?"

"Don't know, yet." Luke added, "Thank you for the phone call. It no doubt saved her life."

"I pray that is the case. We need to trust in the Lord. Through Him all things are possible. What exactly happened after I talked to you?"

"I rushed to Caroline's home, with an unwanted police escort, I might add. As it turned out, having the entourage was instrumental in helping me get emergency medical help. We found her in a semi-comatose state. From the way it looked, she had overdosed on sleeping pills. How many she ingested, we don't know."

Father Jonathan shook his head. Luke asked, "I'm curious as to how you knew she was..." Tears filled his eyes, and he was unable to speak. Finally getting a grip on his emotions, he wiped his eyes and continued, "She came to see you for an exorcism, didn't she?"

"Yes, but *why* she didn't say, and I didn't press it. Guess now I should have. She came back, today, with some cock-and-bull story about a sorority sister who opted to give her brother a kidney, aware she would not, in all probability, survive the surgery herself. She wanted to know if giving one's life to save another was a mortal sin. Red flags started shooting up all over the place. In retrospect, I would have stalled her long enough to keep her with me until I could summon a suicide prevention team member I play golf with."

"Caroline has been under an awful strain and has been quite private about the events in her life since the accident. She didn't want people to think she was going off the deep end. I'm not sure there was anything you could have done differently." Luke studied his fingernails.

"How bad could it be to drive her to this?" Father Jonathan asked.

"Pretty bad, Father. Pretty bad."

"I couldn't remember your name so I had to call Father Patrick Murphy, and it took some time to sort it out. I prayed you would get to her in time."

"Me, too," Luke jammed his hands in his pants pockets, turning his head away as fresh tears formed.

Father Jonathan placed his arm on Luke's shoulder. "Are you at liberty to tell me what pushed her to go this far?"

Luke cleared his throat. "If anyone deserves an explanation, it would be you." He sniffed. "Forgive me. Usually, I'm not so emotional."

"There's nothing to forgive. It is obvious you care a lot for Caroline, and if you were not so concerned, I would worry about the relationship."

"Well, I may be breaching Caroline's confidence and committing ethical violations with regard to my profession by responding to your question. But, you're already involved and may be better able to help Caroline, if you have all the facts.

"About eight months ago," Luke began, "Caroline and her husband, Grant, were involved in an automobile accident. Doctors Stephen and Eleanor Monroe came upon the scene, as soon as it happened. They determined Grant was all but dead, but they could save Caroline with a transfusion to support her until Helovac could arrive. They rigged up a transfusion line between the two and did, indeed, save Caroline with what blood they could squeeze from Grant."

"How were they sure the blood would match?"

"Dr. Stephen Monroe just happened to be Grant's physician, and he knew Grant had Type O blood, universal. In fact, Caroline told me that Grant had given Stephen the tickets to the symphony that same day. It turned out to be a life-saving gift."

"I see," Father Jonathan said, as he crossed himself. He cocked his head. "Pray, continue."

"You may be familiar with the studies that show sometimes the recipient of a transplant, or in this case a transfusion, can inherit some of the characteristics of the donor. Well, this is exactly what happened in Caroline's case. Grant's spirit has been haunting her ever since she got home from the hospital. Grant was an accomplished pianist and he wants to continue to perform through his wife. He apparently has a burning desire, in his words, to set the world on fire with his music, and the only way that can occur is through Caroline.

"Oh, my God in heaven," Father Jonathan said, looking heavenward. "Although I believe in miracles, I am skeptical when I hear stories such as the one you just related. How can it be?"

"Grant appears to Caroline in her dreams and gives commands. When he wants her to play, he puts her in a trance, and she becomes his alter ego. She has played twice in public, unwittingly, of course, but with such conviction and ability that no one is the wiser. She says she is helpless to resist."

"Hmm." The priest rubbed his chin in thoughtful reflection. "So, how is it Caroline thinks by dying she would be giving her life to save someone, if Grant is already deceased?"

"Good question, Father, but you need to hear the rest of the story. Ironically enough, her father had a heart attack and almost died when he dislodged the oxygen from his nostrils after he was released and went home. Caroline was there at the time and, thankfully, having discovered what had happened, was able to reinsert the oxygen into his nostrils, otherwise, he probably would have died. Caroline was certain that her father had not dislodged the oxygen tubes. She asked me if Grant could possibly have been responsible for the oxygen failure."

"Could he have?"

"Spirits have been known to move small household objects. In fact, Caroline kept losing her car keys and then finding them where she put them in the first place, so, to answer your question, I don't know, but I think it's possible."

Father Jonathan rubbed the back of his neck. "Interesting concept. Sometimes, there's a demonic explanation. Here, I'm not so sure. So, Caroline decided in order to keep someone from being hurt or killed, she would take her own life."

"That's how I see it, in a nutshell."

"Now that I know more about the situation, I can just imagine the desperation Caroline has been feeling. I don't know if she's being brave or foolish. In Caroline's state of mind, who can say? Thank God you got to her in time!"

Their conversation was interrupted when a doctor, with a stethoscope draped around his neck, pushed through the emergency room door.

The priest said, "Ah, Dr. Kee—"

Luke rushed to him. "How is she? Can I see her?" He jammed his hands into his pockets to keep from grabbing the doctor's coat lapels and shaking him.

"She's stabilized and doing just fine. By the way, I'm Dr. Keeler," the doctor said, extending his hand toward Luke. "Good evening to you, Father Jonathan," he said, looking in the priest's direction. "Doesn't appear we will need the last rites, tonight. At least not for this patient."

"That's always good news," Father Jonathan said, crossing himself.

Luke almost fell to his knees, relieved by the news.

Dr. Keeler, directing his attention to Luke, said, "We pumped her stomach and administered activated charcoal to absorb some of the medication, to reduce the toxic level. She may need some psychological help—apparently this was not an accident. Has she demonstrated a suicidal tendency in the past, that you know of?"

Luke swallowed hard. "No, not outwardly," he replied. "Not until this afternoon, that is. Her life has been turned upside down the past eight months. She has been facing some extraordinary challenges that have pushed her over the edge."

"Hmm, well, we're going to keep her overnight. We'll keep her on oxygen and IV fluids and do blood tests to monitor the levels of medication in her bloodstream. How can we contact you?"

Luke pulled a card from his wallet and handed it to the doctor. "Is it permissible for me to stay here, tonight?"

"Yes, if you would like. You can stay in the critical care waiting room. You won't be allowed to see her until tomorrow, however."

"I can live with that."

The doctor nodded and backing towards the emergency entrance, said, "She will recover from the overdose—but it's up to you, or someone close to her, to see she gets the other kind of help." He turned and briskly walked away.

Luke called after him, "Thank you, doctor, for saving her life."

The doctor waved an acknowledgement, as the automatic doors to emergency closed behind him.

"Luke, do you want me to stay with you?" Father Jonathan asked, as he watched Luke sink into the soft cushion of a chair and bury his head in his hands.

Looking up, Luke exclaimed, "What? Oh, no, thank you, Father. You have other souls to save and should be getting back on the job. Thank you for your support and concern. Please continue to pray for Caroline. And me." Luke rose and embraced the priest, who returned the hug before hastening toward the parking garage.

AFTER THINKING about it, Luke decided to spend the night in the waiting room adjacent to critical care, where he felt closer to Caroline. It was late, and he was exhausted. He leaned back and stretched his legs out and was soon fast asleep. The next thing he knew it was 6:00 o'clock the next morning, and he was awakened by the changing of shift. Luke groaned when he sat up. His body protested after being scrunched up in a chair all night. His injuries didn't like it much, either. As he was rubbing his calves, a nurse's aide walked by.

"The cafeteria is open, if you would like to get breakfast," she told him.

"Thank you. Um, nurse?"

"I'm just an aide, but how may I help you?"

"Do you know how Caroline Alexander is doing, this morning?"

"No, but you're welcome to go to the nurses' kiosk. The nurse on duty has the charts, and she can help you."

"Thanks, again," Luke said, and hurried off toward the kiosk.

"Well, good morning," the on duty nurse greeted him.

"Good morning, Stella," Luke replied, looking at her name tag. "Would you please tell me, how is Caroline Alexander doing?"

After pursuing the chart, Stella looked up and asked. "Are you her husband?"

"Just a good friend."

She squinted a long moment at the bedraggled man, and finally said, "Her vitals are good, so it looks like she's turned the corner."

"Thank God!"

"Hey, it's going to be all right," Stella put her hand on Luke's shoulder. "I would guess the doctor may let her go home. Even as soon as this morning. You can't see her until after breakfast and the morning routine. Why don't you go get some coffee? Looks like you could use some. Come back in an hour or so."

Luke nodded and turned toward the bank of elevators.

"The café is on the ground floor, and to your left." The nurse pointed in the direction of the elevators. "There's also a restroom there, where you can freshen up."

"You're a saint, Stella!"

"So, I've heard."

WHEN LUKE returned from the cafeteria, Stella jerked her head in the direction of Caroline's room. "You can see her, now," she said, resting her forearms on the kiosk counter.

Luke squeezed Stella's arm, as he hurried past on his way to Caroline's room. He stood outside her door for a second before pushing it open. Caroline was propped up with several pillows positioned behind her back. She was sipping some orange juice and looking vulnerable. Her hair had been put up into a ponytail, which made Luke's heart melt. When she saw Luke, she put the juice on the nightstand and opened her arms, welcoming him. He rushed into her embrace and pressed her to him.

"I thought I lost you," he cried.

"Oh, Luke. I'm so sorry. That was such a foolish thing for me to do. I've been so desperate, and when I thought of you and Dad being victims, I just couldn't let it happen, anymore. Please forgive me."

"Shh, no need to go there. You're okay, and that's what matters."

Caroline clung to Luke and wouldn't relinquish her hold on him, even when he tried to straighten up.

"Hey, you're pretty strong, but I've got a crick in my back and tender ribs. Don't recommend spending the night in a hospital waiting room chair."

"Oh, you monkey. You spent the night, here?"

"Damn straight, as you would say. There was no way I would leave before I was certain you were going to recover."

"I'm so ashamed." She reached for a tissue.

Just then the door swung open, and Dr. Keeler entered the room.

"How's our patient, this morning?" he smiled. He took his stethoscope from around his neck.

"A bit groggy." Caroline quickly dabbed at her teary eyes.

"Well, that's not a surprise," the doctor said, as he examined her. "Your vitals are good, and you look much better. Do you feel well enough to go home?"

"YES, yes, I do. How soon may I leave?"

"Is there someone that can stay with you for twenty-four hours?"

"Yes," Luke interjected. "She can stay with me."

Caroline looked up at Luke, and he winked at her.

"Okay, then." The doctor tapped his pen on the clipboard. "Hmm, I don't see any reason to keep you any longer than it takes to get you released. I'll have Stella get right on it. It'll probably be an hour or so. Think you can hang on that long?" the doctor teased.

Caroline smiled in reply. Luke stood by. He was also smiling.

After the doctor left, Luke pulled a chair up next to Caroline's bed. He took her hand. "Caroline, I don't want to chance losing you, again. Would you consider moving in with me, until we get this matter resolved?"

"Luke, that's the nicest offer I've had this lifetime, but I can't run away from the situation. I'm determined to face it head on and deal with it to conclusion."

Luke thought for a moment before he asked, "Do you have a plan in mind?"

"Not yet."

"You sound determined. Is it okay if I stay with you a few days just to satisfy myself you're going to be all right?"

"Of course."

Nurse Stella entered the room with a sheaf of papers in her hand. When the final form was endorsed, Stella said, "I'll have copies ready for you at the nurses' station. Stop by before you leave."

"We will. Thank you, Stella," Caroline said. Stella shrugged, as if it was no big deal.

After the nurse left, Luke turned to Caroline. "What can I do to expedite your getting ready to leave?" he asked.

"Just stay close. I'm going to change in the bathroom and will be ready in less than five minutes."

"Are you steady on your feet, or do you need help?"

"I'm okay. I had been up before you came in and did just fine." Caroline swung her legs over the bedside and slipped into her shoes before she headed toward the closet. After retrieving her clothes, she looked back at Luke, "I'll be right out."

"And, I'll be right here."

ON THE drive home, Luke said, "Caroline, we had to break one of your windows to get into the house yesterday. Will you be okay if we stop to get a replacement glass so I can fix it?"

"Yes, of course. If you don't mind, I'll wait in the car."

Luke pulled the Range Rover into a glass shop and got out. Fifteen minutes later, Luke was back, carrying a paper sack. He opened the backdoor and set the supplies on the floor.

"We're all set," he said, and gave Caroline's shoulder a squeeze before fastening his seatbelt.

"That didn't take long. I've just been sitting here thanking God for giving me a second chance to make my foolishness up to those I love so much." Hot tears ran in rivulets down her cheeks. She said, through sobs, "It never occurred to me that by taking my own life, I would be hurting you and Dad and probably Paul, more than Grant ever could."

"You have no idea," Luke said. "My world almost died, yesterday."

AFTER PULLING into Caroline's drive-way, Luke took her elbow and supported her, as they climbed the steps leading to her front door.

"Boy, it's good to be home," Caroline proclaimed, as they entered the foyer. She lovingly ran her hand along the table, as they headed for the drawing room. Luke looked cautiously around before they crossed the threshold into the drawing room. He said, "Do you want to rest, while I repair the broken glass?"

"I should lie down; I'm not as strong as I thought."

"I'll help you up the stairs."

"No, I would rather just lay here on the sofa where I'm close to you."

Scanning the area, once again, Luke asked, "Can I get you anything before I start?"

"Nothing I can think of, thank you for offering." Caroline lowered herself onto the couch and reclined.

Luke fluffed the sofa pillows behind Caroline's back and kissed her on the cheek, and then went to the French door to start the repair. It wasn't long before Caroline drifted off.

IT SEEMED to Caroline she'd just fallen asleep, when she was jolted awake by loud piano playing. She and Luke exchanged alarmed looks. He picked up a hammer and dashed to the piano, looking like he was going to smash it to pieces.

"Wait! Luke, I need to handle this." She clenched her teeth and rose from the sofa. Stomping to the piano, she slammed the key cover down. Standing with her hands on her hips, she shouted, "GRANT! It's over! It's done! I WON'T HAVE IT! DO YOU HEAR, NO MORE! No matter what you do, I will resist. I will not allow you to take over the life that God gave ME!" Caroline paused to catch her breath. "I'm sorry you died so young, but I had nothing to do with it. Remember, I wanted to get a hotel and wait the storm out, but you insisted you could handle it.

"You told me you're the only one that could end this curse so, damn it, do it! I've begged and pleaded with you to let it go; now I'm demanding it! It's you that won't win, I promise you that!"

Luke approached and put his arm around Caroline's shoulder. She was so angry, she shook it off.

"Grant, you're a coward. You pick on the helpless. You almost killed my father and then Luke. Even though you didn't force me to take the pills, it was because of you that I did. You've managed to destroy the love I once felt for you with your relentless obsession, and you will eventually destroy me, if you continue your quest. And, if I do succeed, the sin will be on your head, not mine. Do you want to enter eternity with that kind of baggage? I certainly hope not."

Caroline took great big gulps of air. Suddenly, she was spent. She sat down on the piano bench. Luke sat down beside her. He seemed in a trance, as soft words came from her lover's mouth, in Grant's voice.

"Caroline, I release you. Forgive me, darling, for all of the anxiety I caused you. You're now free to follow your own dreams." The room became eerily silent.

Suddenly, the patio doors swung open, and the long gossamer curtains floated out in a swirl. Luke shook his head and then looked up, as a light breeze engulfed the couple.

"I may be imagining things, but does it seem really peaceful in here?" He gazed at Caroline. Her eyes held wonder, too. She was watching the curtains float, as if on invisible wings.

"Is he gone, do you think?" Caroline walked to the open door.

"Did what I think happen, happen?" he asked.

"I hope so."

"How can we know for sure?"

MOVEMENT FOUR
FINALE

Caroline, I think he loved you enough that when he realized all the pain he had been causing you, he was willing to give up his hold on you and your life."

"If only I could believe that. Let me stay alone, tonight, to test your theory."

"I won't leave you. The doctor exacted a promise from me, and I intend to keep my end of the bargain. Besides, it pains me when we're apart."

"I know; me too. However, if it's truly over, I need to know, sooner than later. Don't you understand, every minute I'm under this curse is devastating? I need to be alone in order to encourage him to appear, if he still persists. I need to be sure Grant has given it up."

"Can I trust you not to, you know?"

"Yes. I give you my word of honor."

"Since it's so important to you, but against my better judgment, I'll leave you here, alone." After a slight pause, Luke said, "Looks like a storm is brewing."

"That's okay. In fact, that's perfect. If Grant is going to persist, the storm just adds more credibility to your theory if he doesn't appear."

Luke had no intention of leaving Caroline alone. He would pretend to leave, and then park somewhere near, where he could watch the house. *Yep, a lotta good that will do. How would I know what's going on inside? Well, at least I'll be close in the event I detect anything going awry.*

Luke picked up his tools and walked toward the door.

"I hope you understand, Luke, I've got to do it on my own. I don't think he will appear if you're with me, especially after what happened, earlier."

"You're probably right," Luke bent and kissed her lightly on the lips. She kissed him back.

"Don't worry. He won't physically hurt me, and I won't let him mentally hurt me, anymore. If he hasn't departed for good, we'll know. Then, we will deal with it. You mean so much to me—you give me strength and hope and I don't want to lose that, ever." Caroline opened the door, and Luke went out into the cool evening.

Luke stood on the portico looking at the closed door. *I suppose she's right. We need to know.* Rain began to splatter the walk, and he jogged back to the Range Rover parked in the driveway. He backed out of the drive and circled the block looking for a good vantage point. He decided to park two houses away, across the street.

Luke had a good view of Caroline's mansion from his vantage point. He turned off the engine and settled back for what he expected to be a long night's vigilance. When evening turned into night, Luke watched, as Caroline turned off the lights in the lower level. Her bedroom light was the only light in the house, for a time. After she turned that light off, he could see tiny glows from night lights around the house: in the foyer and the little light that illuminated the doorbell on the portico. Luke slid back against the seat and folded his arms across his chest. The waiting had begun.

THE NEXT morning the sun poured into the Range Rover. Luke stirred and groaned, and then came instantly awake. *My God, I drifted off.* He looked at Caroline's house. Everything appeared to be normal. He didn't want to admit to Caroline that he stood, or tried to stand, sentinel but he had to know if she was all right. Although it was barely 6:00 a.m., he took his cell phone from his pocket and dialed her number.

"Lo," a sleepy voice answered, on the other end of the line.

"Caroline, it's Luke. Everything okay?"

"Luke. Nothing happened last night, I guess. I slept the whole night without waking up and, I didn't take any sleeping pills."

His voice cracked when he spoke. "That's, well, that's fantastic news. Do you feel any different? That is, I mean when we had our last encounter with Grant, we perceived he was gone."

"Like I said, I slept through the night and haven't had time to assess my feelings. Would you like to come over? I'll have breakfast waiting."

"Yes. In fact, I'm on my way as we speak. Five minutes."

"Five minutes? Where are you?"

"I just pulled into your driveway."

"How'd you get here so fast? Wait, were you out there, all night?"

"Yes, I couldn't leave you. You knew that, didn't you?"

"I suspected as much. I'm on the stairs, but don't expect me to look presentable."

"Like I care what you look like. I'm on your door step but, don't expect me to look presentable, either. I had a rough night."

Caroline ran down the rest of the stairs and swung the door open and embraced Luke like never before. "You monkey, you stayed out there, all night?"

"Only because I care what happens to you."

"And, I care what happens to you." She took Luke's face into her hands and examined every wonderful aspect of it. Tears still streaked his face, but his smile beamed! She thought of all they'd been through over the past months, and how he'd never given up on her, or on helping her. That was something she'd never experienced before. She kissed his lips, and then said, "If you won't say it first, I will. Luke, I'm in love with you."

Tears of joy slid down his cheeks. He slapped at them in embarrassment. "Seem to have gotten something in my eyes," he said. He picked her up and carried her back into the foyer.

"As if you didn't already know, I'm madly in love with you and have been from the first day I laid eyes on you. You're irresistible, and I can't imagine what my life would be without you. You're my dream come true."

He put her gently down and kissed his "dream." After a few minutes, Caroline wiggled free from Luke's grasp. "This is all so very wonderful, but I didn't take time to use the bathroom when you rang the doorbell and—and I gotta go!" she shouted, as she headed back up the stairs.

Luke called to her, "Don't take too long! Wait, I'm coming up after you!"

Caroline shrieked and stepped up her pace.

CHAPTER

15

Before breakfast, Luke asked, "Okay if I take a quick shower? I feel pretty gritty from spending the night in the Rover."

"Of course. You know the drill. The guest bathroom is all yours. Breakfast in thirty minutes."

After breakfast, Luke said, "Caroline, I have to go to the office. I haven't been there for a few days and need to check my messages and calendar."

"I'd like to go with you, if you don't mind?"

"If I don't mind? Are you kidding me, there's nothing I'd like better. Well, at the present time, anyway."

Caroline blushed as she said, "I'll be ready is two seconds."

When they arrived at their destination, Luke said, "I'll park at the apartment and after I check the office, we can take a walk around the Square."

"Perfect. I'd like that."

The sidewalks were still damp and the air was humid. Luke and Caroline strolled hand-in-hand through Jackson Square, enjoying the quiet of the morning.

They turned a corner at Decatur and Caroline shouted, "LOOK, Luke, there's the card reader." Caroline grabbed Luke's hand and pulled him towards the gypsy's booth.

"Yes, there she is," Luke said. Distain dripped from his voice.

The gypsy looked up, as they approached. She displayed her familiar wide, gap-toothed grin, while gesturing them towards the chairs.

"Caroline, I don't think this is such a good idea," Luke whispered.

"Oh, Luke, if Grant is truly gone, the cards will reveal it."

"Well, I don't put a lot of credence in what the cards reveal."

"Please, I want to do this."

"I'm helpless to resist you but, against my better judgment, okay."

They sat down, and Luke pulled his wallet from his hip pocket and took out another ten dollar bill. He placed it on the table. The gypsy looked at the proffered payment and then pointed to her placard. A freshly painted slash of red paint revealed the new cost for a seven card reading was $15, not $10. Luke sighed and took an additional five from his wallet and placed it on top of the ten. The gypsy snatched up the money and, as she had done before, held it to the light. Satisfied the money was genuine she stashed it in the depths of her ample bosom. With the financial part of the transaction complete, the gypsy picked up the cards and handed them to Caroline to shuffle.

Caroline was trembling, as she performed the task. Luke touched her arm and asked, "You sure you want to do this?"

"I have to, Luke." Then, she handed the shuffled deck to the gypsy and sat back with her arms folded. A stoic Luke watched the process unfold.

The gypsy took the cards and placed the deck face down in front of her. She seemed to be enjoying the drama taking place on the other side of the table. Slowly, she flipped the first card over and placed it at the front of the deck for all to see. It was *The Star*.

She looked at Caroline for a long moment before she said, "This is a very good beginning. *The Star*, when not reversed or upside down, means fresh hope and renewal. It also signifies healing of old wounds and spiritual love. A mental and physical expansion, as well as fulfillment and inspiration."

Caroline grabbed Luke's hand. He raised his eyebrows, and Caroline could see his resolve was cracking.

"I'm confused," Caroline said. "When you read my cards before, *The Star* had a different meaning, altogether. You said it was something like experiencing some self-doubt, an unwillingness to change and accept new opportunities, and an inability to express one's self freely. So, how can the same card be so different?"

The gypsy met Caroline's eyes. "Ah, yes. There would be confusion. Remember, when I first started this reading I mentioned the card was not reversed, or upside down. If the card is not upside down, it has an entirely different meaning than when it's reversed."

"Oh, I see," Caroline said, and squeezed Luke's hand. "Please, continue. By the way, what is your name?"

"They call me Fatima," the gypsy said in a quiet voice, as she turned over the next card. It was *The Moon* and it, too, was right side up.

"AH HA! Two cards in the positive position back-to-back, and a very nice card, *The Moon*. This card reveals imagination, dreams, and psychic impressions—in a good way. Is there a psychic in your life?" the gypsy smiled, and lifted her eyes to meet Luke's. She turned the next card. Luke shrugged.

Observing the exchange, Caroline said, "Fatima, when I saw you at the market, you told me about an encounter with Grant. Has he channeled through you, since that time?"

"No. I've received nothing from him, since." The gypsy then directed her attention to the next card. "Look! Your third card is *Judgment*, also in the upright position."

Caroline almost squealed. *Maybe, just maybe, things are going to work out. I can only hope and pray.*

Her fingers went to the small gold cross hanging around her neck. *Thank you, God, if this is the end of it. If not, thank you at least for the reprieve.*

"Looks like *Judgment* is also in your favor," Fatima continued. "Changes and improvements are on the horizon, as well as a satisfactory outcome to a specific matter that has been haunting you."

"Oh, Luke. How can the cards know all of this? It truly is divine intervention."

"No, it's not divine intervention, it's—it's esoteric. I think we should quit while we're ahead," Luke suggested. "Things didn't go so well, last time we were here."

"NO! I want the whole enchilada. I have to see this through to the end and, especially now that the cards are being positive."

He shook his head, but remained silent. The gypsy turned over the fourth card, *Prince of the Chariot of Fire.* It, too, was right side up. Luke sighed in relief.

"*The Prince* tells me a very passionate and virile man will support and encourage you. He is of good character, charming, entertaining, devoted, and responsible." Again, the gypsy lifted her eyes to meet Luke's. Luke noticed, but turned his glance away.

"Luke, that's you. The cards know you. Now you can't tell me you don't believe."

But, before Caroline could finish her sentence, the gypsy had the fifth card turned and placed in line with the other four. It was *The Three of Swords* and, like the others, was in the upright position.

"*Swords.* Hmm, a very complicated card. It expresses sorrow and pain, but with a positive view at the end. There is heartbreak, conflict, upheaval, and separation. This must happen in order to make way for that which is to come." Fatima paused for effect.

Caroline thought immediately of her father and could hardly believe what she was hearing. She looked at Luke, incredulously. Luke put his arm around her and, this time it was he who told the gypsy to go on.

"Yes sir, as you wish," Fatima said, in a condescending tone. She turned the sixth card, and it, too, was upright. "Oh my," she exclaimed. "*The World.*"

"What?" Caroline said, apprehension in her voice. "*The World*, is this a good sign?"

"*The World* is a very good sign, revealing that you will have fulfillment of a personal crisis or a series of events in your life. You will accomplish your goal." The gypsy added, "I can see this pleases you."

Caroline was stunned. For the first time in a very long time everything was coming together. *How do the cards know all of this?* She edged closer to Luke. "Luke..." She was too emotional to finish her thought.

"I know, my love." He shifted so he could look directly at Caroline. "Honey, let's not look at the last card. What if it is bad? Let's go. You've received your answer. You tend to give too much credit to the cards, anyway. If the last card is negative, you will dwell on that, rather than the positive aspects of the other six."

"But, Luke." Caroline saw the concern in his eyes. *Not knowing what the last card is will haunt me the rest of my life. I've got to know. Surely he'll understand.*

Watching the couple closely, Fatima moved her hand to turn the seventh card. Caroline held her hand up to stop her. "No, don't, don't turn it over— not yet."

Caroline saw the dejected look on Luke's face. He said, "You won't be happy 'til you know. I know how you are. Since you're so relentless, *I'll* turn the last card over." Luke shot a look at the gypsy, daring her to defy him.

"As you say," she replied, and dropped her hands into her lap.

Luke reached for the deck and took the corner of the top card. He sat for a few moments fingering it between his thumb and forefinger. He finally uttered, "Oh, what the hell," and slid the top card from the deck and slapped it face up on the table. *The Lovers.* He jerked his head up in astonishment, "*The Lovers,*" he sputtered. Caroline just grinned.

Fatima started to speak, but Luke put his forefinger to his lips. "Shush." Fatima remained silent. "I turned the card over so I would be the one to interpret it."

"As you say," the gypsy said.

"*The Lovers*—this card represents harmony and union," Luke then paused.

Caroline said, "That can't be all. Go on with the rest of the meaning."

As Luke started to speak, he noticed the look on Fatima's face and narrowed his eyes before continuing, "The two embracing figures on the face of the card represent Caroline and Luke. Their lives will be forever intertwined and cannot be disturbed. Upon further inspection, I also see marriage in their future and," he smiled, deliberately, "many children. They will live in eternal harmony and happiness. They were meant for each other, and there is much love and devotion between the two of them. The universe wants them to be together and has arranged for it to happen. Nothing will be allowed to come between them."

The gypsy rolled her eyes.

Caroline stammered, "Really, Luke?" she teased, "*Many* children?"

"Well, that can be negotiated." He folded her hands into his. "What about the rest?"

"You're seriously proposing to me?"

"Yep. I'm waiting with baited breath for your answer. I love you with all my heart. In fact, you're the only woman I've ever wanted to share my Saints T-shirts with."

"Gosh, when you put it like that, how can I refuse?" Caroline hugged him.

"I need it in English. Is that a yes, no, or maybe?"

"Sounds like yes to me," Fatima muttered.

Caroline shot her a look. "Let me answer, if you don't mind."

"Okay—go ahead, answer," Fatima said, lowering her eyes and examining her fingernails.

"Okay, I will. Yes! The answer is yes, Luke. I can't see my life without you, not now, not ever. I've never felt this way about anyone. You stood by me throughout this whole ordeal, lifting me up when I was down and cheering me on when I succeeded. We grew together and learned a lot about each other. You're my guardian angel, and I love you unconditionally, now and forever."

Gathering Caroline in a bear hug, Luke whispered, "Oh, Caroline, if only you knew how many times I wanted to hear those words. I swear I will never hurt you."

"Nor will I ever hurt you, I love you, so."

It was about then, the couple noticed Fatima. She looked at them and grinned. "Don't mind me. I'm just the card reader."

Caroline examined the row of cards, and ran her fingers over *The Lovers* tarot card. She started to pick it up, and Fatima swiftly placed her gnarled hand over it. Caroline didn't relinquish it, and after a tiny tug of war, Fatima shrugged. "Eh, there's more where that came from." She made a grand gesture of letting Caroline slip it into her sweater pocket. "Go," she said. "My work is done, here." Caroline winked at her.

She hugged Luke, and declared she was starved.

"I was hoping for something more romantic but... that'll do."

Caroline wrapped her arms around Luke's neck and said, "I'm too weak from hunger to think about romance, right now, anyway."

"You little nymph, where do you store all of those calories you consume?"

"Recently, I've been worrying them off. But, that appears to be changing. You pick a place, I'll eat anything. Make sure it's quiet and private. I want to discuss the 'many children' phase of this new arrangement."

"Ah, yes, the many children. How about some ribs and cold beer at *Mr. B's*? Sound good?"

"Yep, good and messy. But, also noisy. What the hell, the children discussion can wait. Let's do it!" Caroline turned her attention to Fatima. "Thank you, Fatima, for everything."

"Eh," the old woman shrugged.

LATER THAT afternoon, when they returned to Caroline's mansion, Caroline led Luke into the drawing room. Even though Luke tried to restrain her, Caroline lifted the cover to the keyboard and sat down. She began to play. She stumbled through *Chopsticks*, and they both laughed hilariously. They agreed the piano either needed tuning or else somehow Caroline had lost her magical touch.

"Why don't you try?" she said.

"Naw, I don't want to," Luke protested, "I don't know how."

"Ah, come on. Surely you can pick out something. Humor me," Caroline persisted.

Luke looked around, as if seeking an escape hatch. "Well, okay, if you insist." He sat down, stretched his arms and extended his hands, mimicking Liberace. Then, he looked at Caroline with a broad smile and began playing a perfect rendition of *Turn Back to Me*.

Caroline stared at Luke with wide eyes and her mouth open. Luke, noticing the terrified look on her face, said, "Easy darling. I took piano lessons as a child. When you came into my life, I took some refresher courses. I figured that if I was to compete with Grant for your affection, I would have to learn to play the piano."

Caroline rested her head on Luke's shoulder, and whispered in his ear, "Luke, I love you with all my heart, but if you ever scare me like that, again, you're a dead man."

Luke laughed and began singing, as he played:
Turn back to me, you've touched my heart,
Turn back to me, can't be apart,
Turn back to me, I love you, so,
Turn back to me, you're all I know.
Caroline then joined in,
Turn back to me, I love you, so,
Turn back to me, you're all I know.

ABOUT THE AUTHOR

Judith Blevins has spent her entire professional life experiencing the mystery, intrigue and courtroom drama that unfolds daily within the criminal justice system. Her previous experience as a court clerk, then serving five consecutive district attorneys in Grand Junction, Colorado, has provided the inspiration for her stories. Her second novel, *Swan Song*, is a riveting page-turner that holds the reader in excited anticipation. This time Blevins surprises us and pulls out all the stops with a paranormal tale set in New Orleans.